Praise for John L. Swann's second Charlie Chan Mystery
The Tangled String

"Reading *The Tangled String* took me a while because it was so enjoyable I did not want to rush. The book had great characters, the writing style rang true, and the mystery was good.

"This book and Swann's first Charlie Chan novel, *Death, I Said*, are fantastic reads, whether you are familiar with the Earl Derr Biggers Chan novels or not. Chan fans, get thee to a bookseller pronto!"

Eric Caruso

"Mr. Swann has outdone himself with his second Chan mystery. Clever red herrings keep you guessing with perfectly placed wit. I don't know how he tapped into it, but Mr. Swann has found his inner Chan with this one."

Lou Armagno, editor of "The Wisdom Within Earl Derr Biggers' Charlie Chan"

Also by John L. Swann

Charlie Chan Returns Series
Death, I Said
The Tangled String

Nonfiction
From the Mills to Marcy
Meditations for a Baby Stoic

BEYOND MURDER

A Charlie Chan Mystery

John L. Swann

Nicholas K. Burns Publishing
Utica, New York

Nicholas K. Burns Publishing
130 Proctor Boulevard
Utica, New York 13501
www.nkbpublishing.com
nickburns@nkbpublishing.com

First Edition

ISBN 979-8-9991899-2-9 (paperback)
ISBN 979-8-9991899-3-6 (ebook)

The following is a work of fiction inspired by the characters created by Earl Derr Biggers. Any resemblance to actual events or persons, living or dead, is entirely coincidental. While the book's primary setting is the very real San Francisco of the nineteen-thirties, the orphanage was constructed in the author's imagination. All the characters and events descrbed herein are wholly fictitious.

Cover Art by Sarah Swann

*To mystery readers and film fans everywhere
who have made the wise but humble Chinese detective
a world-wide phenomenon
for more than a hundred years.*

CONTENTS

PREFACE

I discovered Charlie Chan through the many films adapted from and inspired by the six novels authored by Chan creator Earl Derr Biggers. As a youthful reader decades ago, I enjoyed the written Chan even more than his celluloid counterpart. Biggers portrayed a more fully realized character than the charming but at times (in my view) two-dimensional movie Chan.

The passage of the character into the public domain several years ago coupled with the 2025 centennial of Chan's first appearance in print inspired the three novels in my *Charlie Chan Returns* series.

Beginning with *Death, I Said* (2023) and continuing with *The Tangled String* (2024) and this third entry, *Beyond Murder* (2025), my intent is to carry on where Biggers left off, building on his timeline with characters and settings old and new.

My goal is to capture something of the flavor of the original Biggers novels in a manner that both the most dedicated Chan fan and the average reader will enjoy.

Chapter One

EXAMINATION CONCLUDED

Once. Twice. Three times a woman's cry bounced off the walls of a long corridor, shattering the stillness of the night.

Seconds passed with no further outcry, and other sounds arose up and down the hall: bodies shifting, voices murmuring. Finally, brisk footsteps rat-tat-tatted on the linoleum floor.

The entreaties had come from room 151, and the door was wide open. A slim figure slipped into the room, advancing to the bedside of its sole occupant. Despite the loud cries moments earlier the patient appeared to be asleep.

Katharine Meadows had been a hospital nurse for thirteen years, the last three of them overseeing the nurses on this ward and the other two on the same floor. This patient's behavior was something new in her experience.

She stayed in the room just long enough to determine that the woman in the bed was indeed sleeping peacefully and breathing regularly, then returned to her station down the hall.

"What's all the fuss about?"

Cleaning matron Marjorie Crandall, mopping her way down the hall, posed the question as she paused to pass the time. Her short, stout figure leaned on the long wooden handle as the mophead's countless long strands oozed a puddle of soapy water onto the floor.

A dark-haired middle-aged woman who appreciated a good story, "Marj" was always ready to trade gossip with the nurses, and the early-morning hours were normally quiet enough for a smoke and a chat.

"Third nightmare since ten last night," the nurse replied as the two women lit cigarettes. "The patient appears to have an active imagination."

"I always have terrible dreams when indigestion takes hold of me," Marj grimaced. "Maybe she's troubled that way?"

"As much as patients complain about our hospital food, I hardly think that it would give anyone a nightmare," Meadows said with a smile. "Least of all a healthy specimen like—" she glanced at her clipboard "—Jane Doe."

"If she's so healthy," Marj rasped through a puff of smoke, "why's she still here?"

"Here" was the obstetrical ward of San Francisco's Lane Hospital, a five-story red-brick pile built in the last century. In recent years it had become attached—in name and in fact—to the Stanford Hospital, a great concrete structure that rose during the Great War.

The Stanford-Lane Hospitals along with a school of nursing and a medical library occupied much of the Webster Street block between Sacramento and Clay Streets.

"Just another charity case mother-to-be, no name, visible means of support or family," the nurse replied. "Her doctor thought it better to keep her until the baby arrives—which could be a week or more, he says."

"And then," she continued, stubbing out the remains of her cigarette in a sturdy white porcelain ashtray in need of emptying. "She'll be with us until the new arrival can be transferred to Edgewood or some other suitable place."

The campus of the San Francisco Protestant Orphanage Society, more familiarly known as Edgewood, had recently added a facility to respond to the growing number of orphaned and abandoned infants.

"Ah, the poor waif," the cleaning woman said, exhaling and squinting through the smoke. The squint was habitual since she never wore glasses at work, and not because of vanity. Even fashionable spectacles would not have improved the appearance of a puckered, weathered visage the color of unleavened dough.

"And her little one, coming into the world in such a way," Marj continued. "Then again," she sighed, " 'tis the way of things."

Nurse Meadows nodded absently.

"Well, what can't be cured must be endured," she replied sententiously. "Without family to look after her, few options are available. All this is out of our hands. And the child will be better off."

"I'm sure all will turn out for the best," the cleaning woman declared, "but I'll likely not be here to see it."

"Not leaving us, are you?"

"Not for too long this time," replied Marj. "My sister's health is none too good, and with little ones still at home she sometimes needs an extra hand around the house. But I'll be back in due course, never fear."

"I'm looking forward to some time away myself," the nurse confessed, "but not till next month, I'm sorry to say." She shook her head regretfully. "In any case I'll miss our chats while you're away."

Marj nodded in agreement, and her face suddenly broke into a broad smile.

"One thing's certain: Walter will keep things spick and span while I'm gone, I have no doubt," she cackled.

The nurse responded with a wan smile. Walter Jenkins, a slight, elderly custodian, divided his time between his janitorial duties, the nearest tavern, and naps wherever he could find a quiet spot in the hospital.

Marj's laughter became a throaty chuckle.

"Many's the time I've seen the man in one place or another," she began, but her reminiscences were cut short by the ringing of the telephone at the nurse's station.

Dr. Robert Klindleman believed in his work, reveled in it. Ever since graduation from medical school more than twenty years ago he had felt called to welcome the next generation into the world. He looked every bit the successful middle-aged professional he had become: tall, slender, angular features and piercing dark eyes under a furrowed brow, topped by close-cropped iron-gray hair.

The frequent sternness of his expression concealed an underlying benevolent nature. If he occasionally spoke sharply to some of the women in his care, they trusted that it was only in the best interests of their impending motherhood and soon-to-arrive offspring.

The doctor's one professional frustration was the lack of progress in his profession, and his inability to advance the research that he knew would truly make a difference. Toward this end Dr. Klindleman continued to build a successful practice in hopes of pursuing his great dream.

Although he was a skilled medical practitioner, his greater goal was to pursue the intellectual inquiry and pure research that he knew would make a better world.

Dr. Klindleman was a visionary of the first order.

Thanks to years of dedication and hard work his obstetrics practice was one of the best known in San Francisco. Women in the Bay Area recommended him to their friends, sisters and daughters: "Oh, my dear—absolutely! You *must* have Dr. K."

His obstetrics suite occupied a portion of the Lane Hospital building's fourth floor. Patients exiting the elevator turned right to enter a crowded waiting room notable for its bright and cheerful appointments.

On this particular day most of those in the waiting room were patients, a few of them with female companions—mothers, sisters and others. Several of the women looked curiously at the only couple in their midst—partly because men in general were a rarity in Dr. K's waiting room, but also because this man and woman, together, represented something unusual for the time and place.

John Quincy Winterslip and his wife, the former Rose Chan, were accustomed to stares and second looks. They had been married some eighteen months earlier in Boston, where the gathering of their families resembled a kind of miniature League of Nations session bringing together the cultures of East and West.

The Winterslips were an old and respected New England clan, and as a young man John Quincy had ventured west to carve out a career and a life very different from the wealth and social position the family enjoyed in Boston. Previous generations of Winterslip men had preceded him, and John Quincy had partnered some years ago with an older cousin, Roger Winterslip, in his San Francisco business.

While John Quincy had gone west in pursuit of happiness, Rose Chan had traveled almost as far to the east of her Hawaiian birthplace to further her education. The daughter of the well-known Honolulu police detective Charlie Chan and his wife left home to attend university and law school in San Francisco.

There she encountered Winterslip, and they became engaged; their wedding in Boston had followed a year later. Now, Rose would soon complete law school, and she and John Quincy were eager to embrace parenting even as the prospective mother prepared to launch a legal career in San Francisco.

The new arrival would be the first grandchild for both families, and telegrams had flown back and forth between the young Winterslips in California and the two grandmothers-to-be: Chan Chun Shee, in the little house on Honolulu's Punchbowl Hill, and Grace Winterslip, in the storied family residence on Boston's Beacon Hill.

The couple had become accustomed to the doctor's waiting room in recent months. Always accompanied by John Quincy, Rose had visited Dr. K. at regular intervals; not so much for her own peace of mind, but to help reassure her distant mother-in-law. Today's visit, she hoped, would be the last before what Grace Winterslip insisted on calling "the blessed event."

The examination concluded, the doctor ushered his patient and her husband into a consulting room where they took seats on straight-backed chairs. With stethoscope hanging from the side pocket of his white coat, Dr. K. perched on the edge of his desk and delivered a welcome report to the prospective parents.

"Mr. and Mrs. Winterslip, I'm happy to confirm that all is well. Everything is just as it should be, and you can be sure that things are taking their natural course."

John Quincy, a dapperly clad man in his mid-thirties, patted Rose's shoulder reassuringly as she smiled and nodded at the medical man. Dr. K. rose from his seat, drawing the visit to a close with a final remark.

"Just keep observing all the precautions we've discussed and take plenty of rest—and please stay off your feet as much as possible! Any questions?"

John Quincy turned inquiringly toward his wife, a petite woman in her twenties whose flowing blouse-and-skirt ensemble did not entirely conceal her advanced condition. She paused before addressing the doctor.

"Only the question that everyone must ask you," she smiled. "When?"

The doctor returned her smile and delivered a reply in his standard professional demeanor.

"That *is* what everyone wants most to know," he chuckled. "Unfortunately my answer to you is the same one I must give to practically all my patients. 'Soon' is hardly a reassuring word, but given the number of weeks that have passed since I first saw you and all over indications, it's the best single-word summary of your situation."

"I know, I know," Rose replied, sighing. "It's just that I'm so—uncomfortable."

"Completely normal, I assure you," Dr. K. replied perfunctorily. He opened the door of his consulting room, smiled at Rose and shook hands with John Quincy. "I'm sure I'll be seeing you again—soon."

John Quincy Winterslip considered himself a modern and attentive father-to-be. For months he had doted on Rose as the couple prepared to welcome their firstborn.

The Winterslips lived in one of the city's newer and still developing neighborhoods, the Sunset district. They had been fortunate enough to buy a Rousseau house, one that looked from the outside like a small Spanish castle.

Inside, the couple had opted for a more ordinary but comfortable theme that included a nursery. A convenient ground-level garage housed John Quincy's roadster, but most work-days he walked a few blocks to patronize the Lincoln Way streetcar line.

Relaxing at home after seeing Dr. Klindleman, the expectant parents' planning for dinner was interrupted by the doorbell.

"Could you get that, dear?" Rose was consulting a cookbook at the kitchen table but her mind was elsewhere, and on the topic of feeding infants the book had nothing to say. She smiled, remembering her mother's tried-and-true methods of preparing food for her and all her siblings. The second of the Chan family's eleven children, Rose had grown up in a house where a new brother or sister arrived regularly.

"Rose!" John Quincy called.

He joined her in the kitchen, a telegram in his hand and a broad smile on his face.

"You'll never guess who's coming to see you."

"Me? Who?"

"More than one 'who,'" teased John Quincy, "and they'll be here tomorrow."

Chapter Two

NODS AND MURMURED PLEASANTRIES

O f the more than seven hundred passengers aboard the *Monterey* during this particular voyage, more than a few had spent several weeks on what some of them thought of as a floating hotel, one far superior to many an earthbound hostelry.

These mostly seasoned travelers had boarded the Matson liner in Melbourne for the full run, visiting more than a half-dozen ports of call along the way including Pago Pago and Fiji before approaching their final destination.

Others on the *Monterey* made shorter trips along the route, and the popularity of the latter legs of the journey typically filled first and second class quarters to capacity. (The ship offered no third or tourist class accommodations.) Such was the case on this run.

This evening as the ship neared journey's end in San Francisco a number of passengers enjoyed one last promenade on deck despite the foggy, chilly weather. Among them, Clarence Notley walked confidently with an air better suited to someone of higher rank.

The crisp white uniform from head to toe did inspire a certain amount of confidence in the wearer and some of those he encountered, but his visor-cap was plain—unadorned by any indication of rank. In fact he served as assistant chief steward, a combination clerk-waiter-manager, a kind of dogsbody under the watchful eye of the chief steward.

Some of the crew had dubbed him "Naughty Notley," an ironically inappropriate nickname for such an upright and dutiful man who, it seemed, could do no wrong.

Neither tall nor short, Notley was blond-haired, blue-eyed and almost as pale as his uniform. In performing his duties he came and went as quickly and quietly as the recurring feeble growth on his upper lip, which never achieved the status of a mustache despite repeated attempts to cultivate it.

To most passengers he was just another uniformed member of the crew, efficient and deferential. It was unusual for him to initiate a conversation, but he did so from time to time when inspiration struck. Notley valued the routine of the *Monterey*'s regular run to which he was accustomed, even though occasional departures from it were necessary.

Over the last few days he had become acquainted with one of the passengers who had boarded at Honolulu, a handsome man in his late twenties who now stood at the railing smoking a cigarette and watching the horizon for a first glimpse of the mainland. *Good enough fellow for a Chinese, or Hawaiian or whatever he is*, Notley thought, lighting a cigarette and joining him.

"Greetings, Mr. Notley," the passenger said. "There's a chill in the air this evening." Wearing a light-gray sack suit and dark snap-brim fedora, the speaker shivered slightly; he was used to warmer weather. The assistant steward nodded.

"No doubt you feel the change in climate! Is this your first trip to the mainland, Mr. Chan?"

Henry Chan shook his head.

"I went across the country by train to New England year before last, but I thought this trip would be warmer," he confessed. "I guess my optimism failed to recognize that we're preparing to dock in *northern* California." He blew a small cloud of smoke skyward. "But I'll adjust.

"You, on the other hand," he turned to the officer, "you must be used to any kind of weather—anything from San Francisco to Pago Pago."

Notley nodded. "You get used to it. It's part of the job on this run. Sometimes, though," he said, "the thought of settling down somewhere that's always warm is very appealing—*your* hometown, for example."

Henry Chan shrugged.

"Honolulu is not exactly the paradise you've read about in the travel brochures," he replied. "Especially when it's really all you've ever known—"

"Young fellow like you," Notley interrupted, "probably anxious to see some other spots on the map."

The conversation paused as the two exchanged nods with an elderly man who passed by, his gait unsteady. He was followed by a couple; Notley recognized them as a Mr. and Mrs. Perkins. Their brisk pace took them past the slower man in short order, and they were followed by a matronly woman with three chattering youngsters in tow.

Henry looked casually at the little parade, noting how the individuals faded into the mist and fog as the murmur of their voices receded. The older gentleman paused and put a hand on the railing to regain his balance before continuing. The matron spoke firmly to her charges, who giggled and ignored her scolding.

Leaning on the rail, Notley exhaled a plume of smoke as he grasped the glowing remains of his cigarette between finger and thumb. "Say, it just occurred to me—Chan, Honolulu—are you related to the detective I've read about, the one who—"

"Yes, that's my father," Henry cut in. It was not the first time this voyage that the family connection had come up and he was used to it. "Charlie Chan is his name. He's an inspector with the police department."

"Well, now, isn't that something!" Notley's face lit up. "Any chance you'll be joining him in San Francisco? I'd sure love to meet him—always been a great admirer of his."

"No, as he often reminds me his job doesn't usually require being away from home," Henry said with a grin. "He says, 'The farther one travels, the less one may know,' but that's Chinese philosophy for you."

Passers-by emerged from and disappeared into the mist in increasing numbers. The woman with three noisy children returned, followed by the man and woman who had strolled by arm in arm earlier. The couple was dressed for dinner, having just come from the captain's table, and greeted Notley with the familiarity of shipboard acquaintance.

"Nice to see you again—Mr. Notley, isn't it?" The man nodded, smiling, his gold-framed eyeglasses shining faintly in the mist. He was average in height and slight in build, about forty years of age, with scanty dark hair combed straight back from a receding hairline. His features were pale and lean: eyebrows, mustache and lips all thin, as though in sympathy with his diminishing head of hair.

"Yes, that's right," the assistant steward replied. He had found Mr. Perkins a genial conversationalist, better than most passengers on this crossing, but Notley thought his female companion withdrawn, preoccupied. *Probably got too much on her mind*, he speculated, before remembering his manners.

"Oh, and this is Mr. Chan of Honolulu—Mr. and Mrs. Perkins of San Francisco."

Nods and murmured pleasantries were exchanged. Modestly dressed in evening wear suitable for dinner at the captain's table, the woman was her husband's equal in age, a little less so in stature. Henry stifled a grin as he realized that the couple bore more than a passing resemblance to Jack Sprat and his wife of the old nursery rhyme.

He was rail-thin while she was jowly and—Henry could think of no better word—portly. She was also rather flamboyant in appearance, her garishly made-up face contrasting with an almost metallic platinum blonde hairstyle, but Notley had noticed during his previous encounters with them that she was often content to let Mr. Perkins do most of the talking. This time was different. Suddenly Mrs. Perkins started, abandoning her private thoughts, and addressed Henry.

"Chan? From Honolulu? Why, surely you must be the famous policeman—"

For the second time that evening, Henry politely set the record straight.

"I think you're referring to my father, the detective," he said with a smile. "I'm Henry Chan."

"Oh, I beg your pardon, I'm sure—that is, I suppose you're used to having someone so well known in your family. Didn't I read somewhere that you have a great many brothers and sisters? It must have been so rewarding, being part of such a large family—all the little children, the hustle and bustle—"

"Cecily, I'm sure Mr. Chan would rather not discuss his childhood with strangers," her husband interrupted with some embarrassment. "Please forgive my wife, Mr. Chan. She and I look forward to starting a family, and the topic of little ones seems to come up at every available opportunity."

Mrs. Perkins hastened to add her apologies, but Henry took the matter in stride.

"Not at all, no need to apologize! I *am* the oldest of eleven, which has been something of an advantage." He grinned. "I suppose I was the favored son growing up since I was the first. Big families—at least mine—have lots of pros and cons for the children. And the parents, too," he added hastily.

"Melvin and I—well, I suppose I do bring up the subject rather more than is necessary," the woman admitted, "a delicate topic for public discussion, at least it was in the past. Nowadays, I suppose it's more common for people to speak openly of such things—"

Notley intervened. Smoothing troubled conversational waters among passengers was one of his many duties.

"No doubt Mr. Chan shares my best wishes for both of you and your future family," the assistant steward said with a smile.

"You're very kind," Mr. Perkins returned graciously. "Good evening to you both. Let's run along, Cecily! Still lots to do before we dock."

The Perkinses departed, and Notley returned to his earlier question.

"You were saying that your father is something of a homebody? I thought he might be working on a case in San Francisco like the one that made the papers a few years back, and maybe you were on your way to see him."

"No, not at all. In fact he's at home while my mother and I—"

A short, stout woman bundled in a heavy cloth coat approached. Her head was topped by a trapper's hat, its earflaps down and firmly secured. Through a bundle of multicolored scarves wrapped around her face, the woman addressed her son familiarly in Chinese.

"Henry! Where is your warm coat and muffler? The cold air and the mist, the spray of the ocean, these cannot be good for you!"

The young man grinned at what was for him a familiar maternal refrain of concern. Only the topic was new, since dressing for cold weather was seldom discussed in Hawaii.

"I'm fine, Mama, really," he reassured her in English. "I appreciate your concern." He indicated his smoking partner. "This is Mr. Notley, a member of the crew—Mr. Notley, my mother."

The woman bowed, and Notley nodded. "Pleased to meet you, Mrs. Chan. Your son and I have been admiring the view." Henry's mother may have smiled politely, but it was difficult to tell since the scarf obscured much of her face. Silence hung in the air like the evening mist, and Notley decided to depart.

"You'll both excuse me, I'm sure." He discarded the very end of his cigarette, dropping it overboard. "There's a lot to do before we dock, and no doubt my boss is looking for me."

Notley smiled at the pair, raised his hand to his visor in a parting salute and sauntered into the murk. Henry watched the uniformed figure recede and wondered what made someone like an assistant steward tick. Encounters with famous passengers must be one of the job's few perks, he thought; hence the interest in his absent detective father.

Henry flicked the last of his cigarette overboard and hastily introduced a new subject. This was a tactical move. He hoped to avoid a lecture on smoking, a "dirty American habit" as his mother called it.

"Shouldn't you be practicing your English? You promised Dad, you know."

Henry's tone was mock-accusatory with a heavy hint of affection. As the oldest of eleven children he loved and respected his parents, but a mischievous spirit often prompted him to chaff them about matters large and small.

"Maybe I speak English better than you someday," his mother retorted, abandoning her native Cantonese. "Already today I speak it better—much better than when you were small."

The family matriarch could hold her own when the older children teased her, and her command of English *was* greatly improved in recent years, Henry admitted to himself.

"If Dad were here he'd probably remind us that he set a good example for you by going to night school, and when he convinced you to take a class with him—"

"Your father is very smart, very smart," she replied, shivering slightly. "If he were here also he would not stay in such cold place with no coat, maybe?"

Henry laughed. His mother had won this round.

"You're right," he agreed, "and he would probably remind us both to go below and pack. We'll be docking sometime in the next several hours, and I know you like to take your time."

"Remember old Chinese saying, 'pulling sprouts up does not make them grow faster,'" she reminded him. "Better to go slow and pack good."

"You win," Henry said with a smile. "Let's go warm ourselves and make sure our trunks are in good order."

Chapter Three

"HOT LIKE HELL"

The wrath of the *Monterey*'s chief steward was like the rare squalls the ship encountered on its regular run: sudden and soon over. At the moment, William "Wild Bill" Craxton was striving to bring order to the last leg of the ship's current run, and he had need of his assistant.

"Notley!" bellowed Craxton, a uniformed, gray-whiskered individual whose face suggested a disgruntled Santa Claus. The summons produced almost immediate results, as Notley appeared in the cabin doorway.

"There you are, you scalawag," Wild Bill fumed. "Where have you been keeping yourself?"

"Just a stroll topside and a chat with a passenger or two," Notley said breezily, lighting a cigarette and leaning on a corner of a small, paper-strewn desk. In private the two men dispensed with the formalities of rank because they saw eye to eye on many things. They had a professional understanding and a kind of master-apprentice relationship.

"A familiar name on the passenger manifest caught my eye, and I wanted to pay my respects. Oh, and the Perkins couple turned up as they always do."

Craxton lit a foul-smelling pipe, a short bent briar that was his constant companion, to conceal his impatience. He had found recently that Notley was getting to be more trouble than necessary.

"Wish that pair would make themselves scarce," he grumbled, gesturing at the messy desk. "While you were socializing I've been trying to put things in order, what with the extra work on this run . . ."

He paused, cocking an eye at the younger man.

"That name on the manifest—old friend of yours, was it?"

"Not quite. A member of a certain family. A well-known name in this part of the world, I'd say."

Notley opened a porthole a few inches to let some of the smoke escape. The cabin's atmosphere was a bit thick, but Craxton was not.

"Ah, I see—a family member of a professional acquaintance? Well, say it out! Who's this mysterious passenger?"

"Let's just say that it's a name I thought worth exploring." He paused for emphasis. "You've heard of Charlie Chan?"

"Who hasn't?" Craxton shrugged and fumbled for matches to relight his pipe. "On this run, seems like everybody knows somebody who knows the famous Inspector Chan. I've never met him. Have you?"

Notley picked up a clipboard and tapped on the sheaf of papers it held.

"Hadn't I better see to these? Harbormaster will be coming aboard soon, and we want all things to be in order."

"You're damned right," Craxton said tersely. "I reckon it's time you were—"

Notley's dismissal was delayed by a respectful knock at the cabin door. A fresh-faced uniformed crewman presented himself, envelope in hand.

"For you, sir, from the captain."

Handing over the note, the crewman departed. Craxton exhaled smokily and scanned the brief communication, deciphering the captain's scrawl.

"Blast the luck!" he exclaimed to no one in particular. "We're laid up here for repairs, 'duration to be determined.' "

Notley scowled and swore.

"That's a spanner in the works," he grumbled. With that, he took his leave.

The chief steward rummaged among the papers on his desk till he located a clipboard thick with passenger manifests, past and present. He examined several and scanned them with renewed interest.

Wild Bill Craxton owed his moniker to a rambunctious youth, but he was no longer as wild as in former days. He shared his innermost thoughts with no one, least of all a subordinate, but he often gave voice to them when no one was within earshot. So it was with his belated reply to the now-absent assistant.

"You'd better watch your step, damn you."

At San Francisco's Pier 32 the arrival of a Matson liner occurred with some frequency. Henry Chan was used to Honolulu harbor's festive "boat days" at which both departing and arriving liners were feted by—it seemed to him—the whole community.

Here it was a different story. This morning's docking preparations, disembarkation, baggage-handling and the hustling, teeming dock itself contributed to a big-city, matter-of-fact, transactional atmosphere unlike a Honolulu boat day's leis, music and hula dancing.

Henry was reminded of his first San Francisco arrival when most of the family were on their way to Boston for Rose and John Quincy's wedding, but he found this morning's scene even more colorful and chaotic than his vivid memories.

The waterfront was alive with thousands of travelers, sailors, longshoremen and workers of all kinds. The sights, sounds and smells of commerce on a grand scale were almost overwhelming, especially for Henry's mother.

"All kinds of people make too much noise for ears of an old Chinese woman," she grumbled, clutching a new suitcase purchased for the trip. "We can go somewhere not so loud now?"

Henry laughed.

"First, when I think of an *old* Chinese woman," he said teasingly, "Empress Lü comes to mind, not you. Second, as soon as our trunks show up we'll look for John Quincy—and I'm sure he'll take us somewhere much quieter."

Henry and his mother along with hundreds of fellow passengers were making their way through the crowd of welcoming family members and friends. The throng moved slowly toward the baggage claim area, and the younger Chan took hold of his mother's arm. *It wouldn't do to lose one's mother in a strange city, even briefly*, he told himself half facetiously. *I'd never hear the end of it.*

"Well, well," a voice from behind them said loudly over the noise of the crowd. "Fancy meeting you both here!"

Henry and his mother turned to see a welcome party of one, John Quincy Winterslip. Mrs. Chan bowed low and Henry grasped his brother-in-law's outstretched hand.

"It's good to see you, John Quincy! How's my sister?"

Winterslip's reply was forestalled, as Mrs. Chan quickly voiced the concern of a grandmother-to-be.

"Yes, please! How is Rose?"

John Quincy was quick to deliver reassurances. He knew full well that Rose's mother felt her older daughter's absence from home keenly.

"She's fine, quite happy and very energetic," he said reassuringly. "I believe she has a bit of the 'nesting instinct,' as they call it, so you'll find our house in perfect order. She was cleaning and organizing even before Henry's telegram came."

Laughing and chatting, the three made their way to the line of baggage claimants. John Quincy suggested he take Mrs. Chan to his nearby car while Henry awaited their trunks.

Assuming his place in a long line of travelers Henry saw some familiar faces from the *Monterey*, including a woman making her way out of the pier-shed accompanied by a porter wheeling a trunk-laden cart. It was one-half of the Perkins couple he had met on the ship.

"Hello again, Mr. Chan!" Mrs. Perkins cried. "All ready for the excitement of the city?" She looked over her shoulder; Henry assumed Mr. Perkins was not far behind.

"I will be as soon as I can get the family luggage in order," Henry replied. "How nice to see you again." He pointed toward the Perkins cart. "Planning a long visit?"

Mrs. Perkins laughed in staccato fashion, raising a gloved hand to cover her mouth.

"Oh, my! You sound just like my husband. He says I pack far too many things and that my trunks are always filled no matter how long we're going to be away." She turned to look toward the front of the line again. "I can't think what's keeping him—oh, there you are, my dear. You remember Mr. Chan?"

Mr. Perkins arrived somewhat out of breath, a single brown suitcase clasped in his left hand.

"Of course! How are you faring, Mr. Chan? Happy to be on terra firma again?"

Henry smiled politely.

"Yes, and I'm very much looking forward to seeing something of the city—once I retrieve our trunks." He paused for an instant, struggling to add further to the conversation. "Mrs. Perkins was just telling me that she's fond of packing very thoroughly for your travels."

Both Perkinses laughed, and Mr. Perkins gestured toward the stacked trunks on the cart. "That's about the size of it! Hardly anything left at home, I imagine. Naturally, she stows away more for longer stays, but still—"

"Just imagine what our luggage needs will be in future," his wife broke in happily, "when our family grows in number. In fact, my dear, we should begin thinking about it soon while the sales are on—"

"Yes, yes, of course," Perkins said hastily. "All in good time. I'm sure Mr. Chan isn't interested in our shopping plans, and we'd best be off before I have to tip this fellow a year's salary for his patience."

The porter's ears perked up at this, and he wheeled the cart away in the wake of the departing couple. Both of them waved farewell to Henry Chan, who returned the gesture as he continued to move forward in the dwindling luggage line.

John Quincy Winterslip made his mother-in-law comfortable in the back of a roomy blue sedan parked not far from the pier, and the two waited for Henry and the trunks to arrive.

Although he and Rose had been married for more than two years, John Quincy suddenly realized that this was his first one-on-one conversation with her mother. Rarely at a loss for words in social circumstances he found himself a bit abashed at the situation.

"Pleasant voyage? No rough seas I trust?"

Seated behind the wheel, he started the engine and turned to face the redoubtable family matriarch in the rear seat of the automobile. She wore the same multiple outer layers of clothing that had protected her from chilly ocean breezes aboard the *Monterey*.

The head swathed in scarves nodded in reply.

"Our weather here must seem a bit brisk compared to the islands," John Quincy said a trifle nervously, silently cursing his tendency to state the obvious. "Shall I turn on the heater?"

A second nod.

John Quincy made the necessary adjustments, hoping that warmer air might help defrost the conversation. The Boston native was used to all kinds of weather and found San Francisco's occasional dips in temperature bracing, but he knew Mrs. Chan had spent very little time away from Honolulu's hot climate.

Determined to be a good son-in-law he turned the heater control to its highest setting, and the sedan interior was well on its way from balmy to stifling when the front door opened.

"Where's the best place for this—front seat or trunk?"

Henry had arrived with a porter wheeling a cart bearing a single steamer trunk.

"It should fit in the trunk," John Quincy replied, exiting the vehicle to assist. "Just the one?"

Henry nodded, tipping the departing porter once the lone trunk was stowed away, and the two men climbed into the front seat of the well-heated auto interior.

"The trunk is Mama's—they weren't able to account for mine," Henry explained ruefully. "The baggage people suggested I return around four this afternoon. They expect it'll turn up by then.

"Say," he remarked, turning toward his brother-in-law. "Isn't it a bit warm in here?"

Before John Quincy could explain, a voice came from the back seat.

"Hot like hell inside this car. Maybe you need to open windows."

After a short uneventful drive and the delivery of mother and luggage, Henry Chan was glad to seek his mislaid trunk and escape the domestic flurry in the Winterslip household. Happy as he was to see his sister Rose, Henry knew that their mother's period of "settling in" would take some time. After constant maternal companionship during the four-day voyage he felt the need of a short break.

Besides, he reasoned, the timing of a brief absence was both opportune and necessary. The expectant mother-to-be and grandmother-in-waiting had much to discuss, and with only a few personal items in his valise Henry really needed to secure the trunk's contents. He asked John Quincy if he might borrow his automobile.

"By all means! Please take the old bus and treat it as your own." John Quincy handed Henry the keys to his "old bus," a late-model sedan as pristine as though it had just been driven off the dealer's lot. "I'll hold the fort here till you return. It won't be hard duty," he continued. "I imagine just staying out of the way should meet the case."

"John Quincy!" Rose called from upstairs. "Could you be a dear and help Mama with her trunk?"

"Be right there!" The dutiful husband turned to Henry and smiled. "See what I mean? Now, off you go. Retrieve your luggage and take the rest of the evening off."

Henry needed no further urging. He took the keys, thanked his brother-in-law and departed. *Just one stop on my way to the pier*, he told himself.

I think it's time to send a wire.

Chapter Four

CALICO JIM'S

Along the waterfront the past lay buried beneath the present. Old East Street was long gone, and with it any trace of the remains of sailing vessels now entombed under dry land.

From China Basin to Fisherman's Wharf, all along the edge of reclaimed land, ran the Embarcadero. The sweeping two-hundred-foot-wide boulevard had been paved just a few years ago and was lined by concrete piers.

The Embarcadero's maelstrom of commerce and traffic, the loading and unloading of goods and persons from all over the world, started well before dawn and lasted for much of the day, but in the late afternoon activity nearly ceased. In the evening hours an eerie calm, often accompanied by the shoreline's famed fog, descended on much of the district.

To reach his destination—the pier-shed in which he hoped his trunk awaited—Henry Chan drove through the district local workers called "the front." This small area off the Embarcadero, bounded by Clay, Drumm and Market Streets, was home to union headquarters and hiring halls for all the workers who plied their trades on the docks or at sea.

Henry noticed longshoremen clad mostly in blacks and whites and striped hickory shirts were much in evidence, as though a meeting had just let out. He was familiar with the sights and sounds of the docks, but this city's shoreline and attendant activity dwarfed Honolulu's more modest workings.

It was almost four o'clock when he parked John Quincy's car on a street within sight of the waning activity, which seemed to be fading with the afternoon sunlight. A few late-arriving passengers for an outbound liner hurried toward a voice crying, "Aboard! Passengers for the *Mariposa*—all aboard."

Walking toward the pier-shed's baggage-sorting area Henry noted with amusement a couple hastily pushing a baby carriage toward the end of a stream of stragglers at the foot of the gangplank. *Hope the baby is enjoying the ride*, he thought. The buggy reminded him that he had yet to present a suitable gift to his sister and brother-in-law for the newest member of the family; maybe a carriage would be useful.

A uniformed clerk found the wayward trunk without delay, and Henry wheeled it away jerkily. He had attached two casters to the bottom in preparation for this trip, but they were no match for sidewalk cracks and uneven pavement. He had stopped and stooped to adjust one of the metal wheels when a voice called his name.

"Mr. Chan, could you please . . . ? Over here!"

Henry looked up from his task and saw Notley, the *Monterey*'s assistant steward, standing in a shuttered building's early evening shadows. The pale man beckoned urgently. Curiosity awakened, Henry wheeled the trunk toward the speaker.

Notley had exchanged his white ship's uniform for a dark suit, topcoat and snap-brim fedora ideal for blending with his shadowy position. His pale face and aspirational mustache stood out in the gloom like a waning moon poking through a murky midnight sky.

"Mr. Notley?" Henry's tone spoke volumes: *What are you doing, lurking in the shadows, and what do you want with me?*

"Yes, yes—please excuse my methods, but I had to approach you in this way—the trunk—because they're watching, and—"

Henry frowned.

"What trunk are you talking about? And who's watching? I don't see anyone here except the two of us."

Notley laughed nervously.

"I tried talking to you on board, but it was too risky. So I arranged for your luggage to be held up so that I could speak to you without—""You *arranged* for my trunk to go missing?" Henry was mystified. "What's this all about?"

Glancing hurriedly over Henry's shoulder, Notley shuddered.

"It's no use," he hissed. "Thought I had given them the slip, but you took your time about getting here. I've got to get back to the ship—been away longer than I should."

His expression was equal parts growing panic and uncertainty. "Maybe this was a mistake."Henry Chan was intrigued, but he was not naive. In many respects he was his father's son.

"Look, I'm here to visit family—not to get involved in this whatever-it-is that you can't explain," he began, "and I'm certainly not inclined—"

"I know, but this is important, and your father—""What about my father?" Henry said quickly.

Notley's eyes darted back and forth, and what he saw behind Henry alarmed him.

"Please, for God's sake! Just meet me tonight at nine at Calico Jim's place, just tell any taxi driver—Calico Jim's—they all know it. I'll be watching for you outside the joint. Please!"

"All right, all right." Henry's patience was wearing thin even as his curiosity grew, and he realized that whatever this fellow's crisis was, a fuller explanation would have to wait. "I'll be there, nine o'clock—"

He turned to look in the direction indicated by Notley's furtive glances, but no one was in sight. The area was deserted.

" —but I don't see why we can't just talk here," Henry said, "Far more privacy here than in some crowded tavern—"

Henry turned back toward the shadowy figure, but Notley was gone.

Calico Jim's was a few blocks off the Embarcadero, half-way down a dingy side street filled with businesses that catered to seafaring men and dockworkers: taverns, outfitters, offices and at least one inauspicious-looking hotel.

Notley's choice for their rendezvous had been called Calico Jim's for many a year, and more than one grizzled patron had passed on the unlikely tale that its founder was *the* Calico Jim, the notorious "crimp" who helped shanghai the unsuspecting and unwilling and supplied them to ship's captains in need of crewmen.

Locals, out-of-town visitors, the savory and unsavory alike—all and sundry were drawn to the dark interior of the old tavern. Patrons could choose to stand and lean against its long wooden bar, blackened by time and traffic, or sit at the wooden tables scattered with rough-hewn benches about the room. With no windows, Calico Jim's main room was always murky—even at midday—since its few bare light bulbs failed to dispel the gloom.

By late evening the tobacco smoke was so thick as it drifted toward the ceiling that Henry Chan saw little difference between the bar's reek and the fog outside once he entered a full quarter-hour after nine. He had kept watch outside as requested but saw no sign of Notley.

Maybe he got tired of waiting, or thirsty, Henry reasoned, *and figured I'd already gone in*. Lighting a cigarette to add to the murk, he made his way through the motley mix of patrons to the end of the bar and ordered a beer.

The barman and proprietor, Jimmy Moran, was a florid-faced sandy-haired Irishman born in County Mayo fifty years ago whose interest in maintaining a certain character outweighed the fact that he had come to the States as a babe in arms. From his outsized personality and thick brogue, first-time customers might think he had just disembarked from a Dublin tramp steamer—an impression he did nothing to discourage. Whether the bar's patrons thought him the spirit of Michael Collins or the legendary Calico Jim himself made no difference to Moran as long as they bought his liquor.

Truth be told, Jimmy Moran capitalized on the dimly lit street and the rundown appearance outside and in (where an old ship's wheel, ropes, pulleys and other seedy nautical relics adorned the taproom walls) to attract all manner of customers, from the socially indifferent to the carriage trade.

The latter had discovered Calico Jim's during the late and largely unlamented Prohibition era, when adventurous flappers and their gentlemen escorts sought out a night-on-the-town "experience." Officially, like many of his professional peers during that peculiar time, Moran operated his business as a "soft drink parlor" for thirteen dry years even as Calico Jim's reputation as a destination for San Francisco's bright young things grew apace.

Despite his sunny demeanor and Irish wit Jimmy Moran brooked no troublesome drunks or jealous romantic rivals eager to brawl. Already tonight he had broken up one fight, and the place was crowded. Still, he was always glad to see an unfamiliar face, especially a well-dressed young fellow such as this current customer. He waited a few minutes, then set a second glass of beer on the bar.

"This one's on the house, young fella—my customary welcome for first-time visitors such as yourself."

Henry nodded and drained the first glass.

"Thanks. How do you know I haven't been here before?"

Moran laid both hands on the bar and grinned.

"Ah, now. Look around—all these, most of 'em, are like family." He gestured at the noisy crowd. " 'Tis a poor excuse for an Irishman who don't know his own kin, and I have a keen eye for an unfamiliar face."

Extracting a damp rag from under the bar he wiped up a small spill and called to an aproned giant of a man wielding a broom near the entrance. Miles Scharvy served as bouncer and general factotum at Calico Jim's, and no one dared complain when he tended bar.

"Miles, mind the bar while I make a newcomer at home—there's a good lad," Jimmy Moran said to his towering assistant, who grunted and assumed a commanding position next to the taps.

"Now, then," said Moran, turning his attention to Henry. "As to your question, it just so happens that one of my regulars asked me to keep an eye peeled for you—Mr. Chan."

Henry was uneasy but kept his composure. His thoughts churned. Notley had made arrangements in advance but to what end? Extinguishing his cigarette, he smiled tightly.

"Since you know my name, what's yours?"

"Jimmy Moran, proprietor of this fine establishment," came the prompt reply. "Pleased to make your acquaintance. To be sure, you must be thinkin' that I'm bold as brass, but—"

"I'm starting to think this is some kind of put-up job," Henry interrupted, his voice cutting through the noise of the crowded taproom. "Where's the man I'm supposed to meet? And what do you have to do with this?"

"Whist!" Moran hissed, glancing around to see if any of his "family" were paying attention. "If you're speakin' of Mr. Notley, doubtless he'll be here soon. Till then, since I've been given to understand that he desires private conversation with you, perhaps you'd be so kind as to join me in the back room.

"You needn't concern yourself overly," the barman hastened to add. "No one will disturb us there, but words intended for two sets of ears need not be shared with two dozen or more."

"Very well." Reluctantly, Henry picked up his second glass of beer and followed Moran to the back of the saloon. The proprietor opened a door and entered a surprisingly large room with chairs and a table on which a deck of cards and stacks of chips awaited some cardsharp's future pleasure.

A bare bulb and long cord depending from the ceiling lit the little table, and a corner floor lamp between two reading chairs cast the two men's shadows on shelving along the opposite wall.

The shelves, Henry observed, contained boxes, unidentifiable cloth bundles (*maybe sailcloth*, Henry thought) and odds and ends. Still unsure of Moran's intentions and the evening's program he was glad to see the rear wall's window, through which he glimpsed an alley and the adjacent building, and a door that appeared to open onto that alleyway.

Moran gestured toward the table.

"Take a pew, Mr. Chan. I'll keep you company till Notley graces us with his presence." The proprietor of Calico Jim's consulted a battered silver watch, drawn from his vest pocket, its chain dangling in the dim light. "Never one to be on time, but he'll surely not be long now."

"I think I'll stand, thank you," said Henry. "I'm not staying long. You haven't answered my question," he reminded his host. "Notley told me that he wants to talk to me, privately. What does that have to do with you?"

Moran looked surprised and a bit hurt.

"Why, I'm a tavern-keeper," he replied, brogue thickening the longer he spoke. "Notley is a good customer, a member of the family as I like to say, and he asked that I keep an eye out for a Mr. Chan, a Chinese gentleman he said you were, and make him welcome in the back room." He paused for breath. "Which I have done, and I surely beg your pardon if I have given offense where none was intended."

Henry stole a glance at his wrist-watch. It was now almost half past nine.

"I suppose that's all right—as far as it goes. But it's nearly nine-thirty and I can't stay here all night as pleasant as the experience is. I'm visiting family, and they'll be wondering as to my whereabouts."

Moran nodded.

"Sure, and Mr. Notley told me you're to become an uncle for the first time. Please to be acceptin' my congratulations in advance of the blessed arrival itself.

"I'll tell you what," Calico Jim's proprietor proposed. "As you're not inclined to wait longer I can deliver a message to Notley if you wish."

Henry frowned. He had no desire to put any information into the hands of this tavern-keeper, but a better idea came to him in an instant. Reaching into his breast pocket he withdrew a small notebook and pencil.

"I wouldn't want to trouble you. I'm sure you're a busy man," he said smoothly, scribbling on a page and tearing it off. "If Mr. Notley should make an appearance tonight or tomorrow please give him this number and ask him to telephone me."

He handed the slip of paper to Moran, who received it with a nod and a smile.

"A fine idea indeed." He pocketed the note and opened the door to the main barroom, whence came the sounds of argument and breaking glass. "If you must go, I'll bid you good evenin' and return to my customers—dealing with such ructions as you're hearing is a nightly duty for the likes of me."

Henry hesitated. Not keen to make his way through the "ructions" he shook his head and pointed toward the back of the room.

"If you don't mind, I'll make use of your rear exit," he said. "I prefer a quiet alley to a noisy tavern."

In an instant Jimmy Moran moved between Henry and the back door.

"Now, then, lad," the barman said with a nervous laugh. "Don't be a chancer—'tis dark as the inside of a cow in that alley, and no moon tonight to boot. Come away, up to the front," he urged. "I wouldna forgive myself if you were to lose your way in the black night."

"O.K., very well then," Henry replied, puzzled by Moran's strong reaction.

Both men made their way through the door and into the main room, where the formidable Miles Scharvy was dragging an unconscious man by his booted feet toward the front door. A second rough-looking customer sat on the floor rubbing his head, his back to the bar.

"Well, now—isn't that fine!" Moran exclaimed in a satisfied tone. "Miles has restored order to the family circle. Are you sure you won't stop for one more, Mr. Chan, on the house?"

"No, I really must be going," Henry said as they walked toward the entrance. "You'll be sure to give Mr. Notley the message?"

Moran opened the cash register with a flourish, depositing the scrap of paper therein.

"You can count on it. I have no doubt he'll be along, if not tonight then tomorrow." The proprietor beamed. "He's a loyal and regular customer, a real member of Calico Jim's family."

"Glad to hear it," Henry managed to reply, with false sincerity. "Thanks so much for—for your hospitality."

Sidestepping Miles, who had just deposited the late combatant on the sidewalk, Henry waved awkwardly at the genial proprietor and made his way out into the misty night.

Chapter Five

AN EXTENDED LEAVE

J ohn Quincy Winterslip thought himself an excellent driver capable of navigating the twists, turns and hills of San Francisco's busy streets. On an average day of professional travel he and his roadster saw much of the Bay area. On weekends he and Rose often motored here, there and up and down the coast. Normally he drove competently—if a bit slowly for Rose's taste.

Today was not a normal, average day for the Winterslips.

It had begun in ordinary enough fashion. Up at his customary time John Quincy had made coffee and was consuming his first cup while perusing the morning's newspaper at the breakfast table.

Rose had risen earlier to fulfill the nesting instinct her husband had noted lately. This morning unwashed items from the night before called to her from the kitchen sink, and she removed the rings from her hands before washing the few dishes.

Drying her hands, she thought again of that last visit to Dr. Klindleman and his single-word prediction regarding her confinement's end: "soon."

"Good morning, my dearest dear," John Quincy greeted his wife, rising from the table to draw back her chair. "Sleep well?"

Rose sat as close to the table as possible, no easy task for a woman in her advanced condition. She shook her head and pushed away the cup of coffee her husband had poured for her.

"Would you care for tea instead? John Quincy inquired. "Perhaps a slice of toast?"

Rose wrinkled her brow. "Nothing right now, thanks," she said uneasily. "I had a restless night, and I think my appetite is sleeping in."

"Maybe you'll feel like eating something a little later when our guests rise to greet the day," John Quincy said optimistically. "You should rest as much as possible and let your mother help out—she seems eager to pitch in."

Rose nodded listlessly. The thought of the family matriarch "pitching in" was both daunting and amusing. Mama had presided over the house on Punchbowl Hill with the same competence and expertise that her detective husband brought to bear on his most challenging investigations. Her elder daughter had mixed feelings about striking a balance in her own household between maternal assistance and Mama's version of martial law. Rose smiled at the prospect.

"Hey, Sis—a bright good morning to you! And to you as well, oh brother-in-law," Henry Chan said cheerily. "Do my nostrils deceive me? Is that the aroma of freshly brewed coffee? Black, please, my needs are simple!"

He gratefully accepted a cup from John Quincy and joined the couple at the breakfast table. Rose sighed at her elder brother's exuberance.

"Please, Henry—we're thankful that you and Mama are here, but the less said about your nostrils the better." Rose's good-natured rejoinder clashed with her pained expression.

"Ah!" Henry replied in a teasing tone perfected over many years of sibling squabbles. "Is the mother-to-be feeling a bit feeble this morning? What can I do to ease your discomfort?"

"I'm fine, just fine," his sister replied, shifting in her chair. "And if I *am* physically feeble, at least it's a temporary condition—unlike someone's feeble mental capacity, which is surely permanent!"

Henry had no quip ready to hand, but Rose didn't wait for his reply.

"So glad that you are your usual charming self, but enough about me," she said. "It's been two days since your arrival, and I've heard practically nothing about your voyage and your traveling companion. That reminds me: I'm surprised Mama isn't awake and taking charge of the household. She's been sleeping quite late these past few mornings—still worn out from the trip, I suppose."

"Perhaps I should call her to the table so that she can negotiate a treaty or at least a ceasefire between brother and sister," put in John Quincy. "Is she normally a late riser?"

"No," brother and sister answered in unison. Henry smiled.

"She's usually the first one awake and up in the house," he said. "I think it may be a few days till she adjusts to the time difference between home and here, and let's just say she was not an early riser on the *Monterey*. Maybe she shares Dad's ocean-going ailment, but I didn't see any instances of—"

"Henry!" Rose paled, and she pushed back her chair abruptly. "Sorry, it's just that I—excuse me." She left the room in haste, a cloth napkin dropping to the floor in her wake.

"I don't get it," Henry said, mystified. "Rose has never been so—what's the dope, John Quincy?"

"The 'dope,' as you so elegantly express it my dear young brother-in-law, is partly a matter of conjecture," Winterslip replied with a slight smile. "Your father would probably have an old Chinese saying to sum up the situation, but I can only offer the following.

"A married man who values peaceful domesticity does not question his spouse's actions. Also, let me remind you that your sister is preparing for an event unique in her experience. In short, whatever the underlying cause of any behavior, including an abrupt departure from the breakfast table, we must remain both supportive and empathetic."

"Got it."

Satisfied with the explanation, Henry helped himself to a second cup of coffee and lit a cigarette, his first of the day.

"When it comes to marriage you're the expert," he grinned. "Of course since I'm the oldest I have some experience of the anticipation of a new arrival in the family, but nothing as up close and personal as a husband's perspective."

"The one thing that I'm still coming to terms with," John Quincy admitted, "is the absolute necessity of accepting that the unexpected will happen, often without any warning at all. At least one has the satisfaction of knowing that—"

John Quincy's satisfied knowledge was destined to remain a secret, at least for the moment. His revelation was interrupted by the abrupt reappearance of Rose in the doorway. Her panicked expression told its own story as she spoke just two words:

"It's time."

John Quincy leapt to his feet, overturning his chair.

"Time? You mean it's—"

"I mean," Rose said, taking a deep breath, "that we should go to the hospital. Now."

"Good lord!" John Quincy cried. "I'll get the car! Do you have your things, your bag? Henry, don't just sit there smoking—never mind, I'll call you from the hospital. Wake your mother and come along when you can, take the streetcar—or a taxi—but don't come till I call—"

The father-to-be's stream of exclamations and instructions continued while he escorted Rose out the front door to the sedan at the curb. Henry followed, but before he could inquire which hospital the automobile sped away. Henry's last glimpse was of Rose reclining on the back seat and a flustered John Quincy behind the wheel, ignoring San Francisco's Uniform Traffic Code.

Henry stood silent for a moment as the car sped away. Suddenly a voice punctured his fleeting thoughts.

"Why do you stand outside staring at the street? Come inside house, out of cold."

Henry's mother stood in the doorway, dressed appropriate-ly for an arctic excursion in one of the multilayered outfits she had worn during their recent voyage.

"Mama—you're awake, thank heavens. I was just coming to tell you—"

His mother smiled, at least Henry presumed she was smil-ing, judging from the tone of her remarks. A scarf concealed the lower part of her face.

"Glad you can see that I am not asleep. Maybe someday you will be great detective like your father. Why you not come wake me for breakfast time with Rose and John Quincy? Never mind," she said dismissively, walking through the house into the kitchen with Henry in tow. "Happy to be awake and not on ship."

She paused, looking at the breakfast table and the over-turned chair before turning to Henry.

"What happened here? Where—" Suddenly her eyes widened as realization arrived. "Rose? And John Quincy? They go to hospital?"

"Yes, Mama," Henry replied. "Rose said it was time—"

"Woman knows," his mother affirmed. "Always. Why did you not go to hospital with Rose and John Quincy?"

"I was waiting for you so that we could go together," Henry said with a grin. "Are you ready?"

"We go now?"

"I'll call a taxi," Henry replied, picking up the telephone.

Two men sat in an office of the Honolulu police station, an elegant stucco building with sandstone and marble trim-mings and massive mahogany entrances. Built within the last decade to accommodate the growing needs of a department established in the previous century, police headquarters had followed in the architectural footsteps of the California Span-ish Style city hall, a veritable palace completed a few years prior at King and Punchbowl streets.

Although their official relationship was that of a supervisor and his subordinate, the two men were at ease in each other's company. The Chief of Detectives had been Charlie Chan's boss through thick and thin: the "thick" of high-profile cases in Honolulu and on the mainland, and the "thin" of more mundane police work on the streets of the growing city.

When he was sergeant of detectives Chan had reported to a less supportive supervisor, the now-retired Captain Hallett. Since those days, promotion and opportunity had resulted in the peripatetic career success that Chan felt was due in no small part to the cigar-smoking superior officer he referred to as simply "the Chief."

Although a cultural divide separated them, years of shared police work and their individual distinctions had established a strong, if imperfect, bond. Each was a different kind of outsider. To many of his Hawaiian officers the Chief was still a *haole*, a white man from the mainland, even though he had lived and worked in Honolulu his entire adult life.

Chan, even though he had been a Honolulu resident for more years than his chief, was Chinese-born and the only Chinese detective on the force. He was neither *haole* nor *kanaka*—native Hawaiian—and had long felt the conflicts between his birthplace, adopted homeland, and the work his more traditional cousin referred to as "your white devil profession."

Always an outsider in his investigations, never part of a majority, Chan had turned "otherness" into an asset, one that he combined with a blend of philosophical wisdom, common sense and intuition. He sometimes attributed professional success to the last of these—"Chinese are psychic people," he often said—but (as the Chief well knew) Chan frequently supplemented deductive reasoning with the best tools available to police science.

His often bland expression concealed wit and determination. Through pithy reductions of Confucian and Daoist philosophy he delivered pointed messages to willing and unwilling listeners, both the innocent and the guilty. Those who dismissed Chan and his sometimes enigmatic maxims as mere curiosities did so at their peril.

A breeze spawned by Hawaii's famous trade winds wafted through the Chief's office window, stirring the papers on his desk. Charlie Chan had been at work early on this particular morning, perhaps in anticipation of the wire that had prompted this meeting with his superior.

He handed the telegram to the Chief, who was enjoying his first cigar of the day.

CHARLIE CHAN, INSPECTOR

HONOLULU POLICE DEPARTMENT

HONOLULU, HAWAII

ARRIVAL GRANDCHILD IMMINENT STOP YOUR PRESENCE REQUESTED SOONEST IF CHIEF PERMITS STOP SUGGEST CLIPPER STOP WIRE TRAVEL PLANS TO

YOUR LOVING SON
HENRY

The Chief smiled broadly as he returned the cable to the detective. Seated in a chair in front of the desk, Chan leaned forward to receive it. The ever-decisive Chief delivered his verdict:

"No question, Charlie—you should go. And I've got a little surprise for you."

Chan grinned. As always he was prepared to act. In this case ample notice to the Chief, albeit necessarily vague as to the exact timing, had been provided some months earlier.

"Thank you for answering the question about leave of absence before it was asked. Happy to say that several days ago I packed a suitcase in preparation for possible summons to mainland. But what surprise do you speak of?"

Plucking a sheet of paper from a stack on his desk, the Chief slid it across to Chan's waiting hands.

"This came yesterday—couldn't find the time to catch up with you then. Just as well, since that telegram seems to seal the deal."

Chan scanned the brief missive, but it was the sender's last name that caught his eye immediately.

Flannery.

"Just to save you some time," the Chief put in, "it seems the San Francisco department would like a little informal assistance from us concerning the shipping of contraband. They know heroin is getting into their jurisdiction in significant quantities, and it seems the trail leads here and beyond.

"This is nothing new for us," the Chief continued. "As you know, Charlie, we're not a final shipping destination for this kind of thing—mostly we're just a way station."

Chan nodded.

"Last big case of similar kind was Captain Hallett's, some years ago," he recalled. "Same involved murder of Dan Winterslip.

"But opium from my ancestral homeland has found its way to unfortunate customers since ancient times, lately in Europe and America. Maybe this is another chapter in the same book?"

"The boys in the lab tell me that modern science has made it easier and deadlier to process the raw opium, turn it into morphine and heroin, and ship the refined product. That's what we seem to be facing now," the Chief explained.

"Our colleagues on the mainland seem to have an idea that we can give them some insight as to the where and how. *Where* it's coming from they think they know, but *how*—they're not so sure."

The Chief thumped the desktop with an open hand for emphasis.

"Bottom line, they think that someone who's traveled the Honolulu-to-San Francisco route can shed some light. And it appears the deputy chief there is an old friend of yours."

Chan smiled.

"Former captain of San Francisco police provided the opportunity for visiting detective to assist in the investigation of Sir Frederic Bruce's murder several years ago," he recalled. "I was happy to renew our acquaintance some time later, again in San Francisco. You will recall attack on Scotland Yard inspector named Duff, here in this building, which led to delivery of the culprit to Captain Flannery on mainland."

"And I also recollect that you acquitted yourself well in both instances, Charlie," the Chief reminded him. "You've got to watch that humility—too much of a good thing sometimes," he said, wagging a finger in jest.

"Better to appreciate the abilities of others than to dwell on mine, I think," Chan remarked. "Old man in China once wrote that humility is one of mankind's three great treasures."

"Some day when we have more time I expect you'll tell me about the other two," the Chief said, "but right now you'll probably want to make some travel arrangements."

Despite the letter and telegram he had half expected his best detective to politely refuse an extended leave. Chan was always reluctant to take time off from his duties because he knew his absence from the small department would burden his colleagues.

"And don't worry about things here in your absence," Chan's boss declared. "The boys will fill in for you, no problem. Maybe one of the younger men will see this as a big chance to solve a case of his own." The Chief smiled at the thought. "Say, what about the missus, Charlie—is she going along with you?"

"Eager grandmother-to-be always one step ahead of events," Chan replied. "Son Henry has already accompanied her to San Francisco on fast boat."

The Chief chuckled.

"I'm not a bit surprised. I'll bet she's keeping Henry busy, too." He drew on the cigar, sending smoke toward the ceiling. "But Great Scott, Charlie, the next Matson liner bound for San Francisco won't sail for several days—"

"Please pardon this rude interruption," Chan put in, "But your keen mind arrives at vital thought with speed of light. My slower brain machinery took longer before coming to the same conclusion, but as Chinese proverb says, 'heroes think the same.' This morning I purchased single ticket for seat on Pan American Clipper that leaves not many hours from now."

"That's fine!" the Chief cried. "Why, that'll put you there on Friday—with luck, you'll arrive before that grandson of yours puts in an appearance."

"Grandson—or perhaps granddaughter, who knows?" Chan replied. "One more Chinese saying: 'When the old man lost his horse how could one know it was not a blessing?'"

Chapter Six

THE LONG CORRIDOR

Rose Winterslip awoke with a start. She was lying in bed in a dimly lit room, and some strong odor reminded her of . . . sick people?

Gradually the recent past came into focus: a quiet morning at home with her husband, that scamp Henry teasing her when she felt unwell, the mad dash in the car to Lane hospital and a barrage of questions. Then—

A murmuring nearby startled her. The voice was that of a woman, a youngish woman, Rose thought hazily. It came from nearby. She turned her head toward the sound.

In the bed next to hers Rose saw another maternity ward case, a woman just about her age also of Asian descent. *A kindred spirit*, she thought. The medical chart affixed to the woman's bed read, "Jane Doe," and Rose could just make out a tiny circle with two curving shapes and dots on its lower-right corner.

"Hello," Rose said sleepily. "Have I been asleep long?"

The other woman's brow furrowed as if she was trying to answer a difficult question without success, but she remained silent.

"My name is Rose, Rose Winterslip. Are you—?"

The other woman's eyes opened briefly, and she looked hazily toward her questioner.

"Rose . . . Chan . . . " She read shakily from the chart on the side of Rose's bed. Although Rose couldn't see the chart she realized how the mixup had happened.

I must have given them my maiden name, she realized, *when they were asking me all those questions.*

In a barely audible voice the woman continued to mutter, uttering a few syllables that Rome thought sounded like Cantonese—words meaning, "bad dream" and . . .

"Demon"?

"Do you speak Chinese?" Rose posed the question in Cantonese, hoping that her limited command of the language was equal to the situation.

Though still groggy Rose had recovered enough to realize that the other woman was dozing off or drifting into unconsciousness. "Are you . . . are you feeling all right? Would you like me to call someone, Jane?"

"*Zou tau*," the whispered reply came, followed by silence. Rose had learned the Cantonese for "good night" at a young age, and from the woman's breathing it was clear that Jane was now asleep. Rose was inclined to follow her example. The effort she had made to focus and talk had tired her.

She closed her eyes and dropped off.

"How are we feeling now, dearie? Better?"

A woman in nurse's uniform appeared, or perhaps two of them. Rose blinked sleepily, her vision as murky as the Bay Area's fogs. In a few seconds the two nurses merged into a single uniformed figure that removed the chart from the side of Rose's bed and placed it on a clipboard.

"I'm—I guess I must've fainted, I don't remember—" Rose was puzzled to see a startled look on the nurse's face. "Is there something wrong? You look surprised."

The nurse wrote something hastily on the chart.

"My goodness, dearie, you gave me a start! A note here on your chart says, 'Miss Chan speaks only Chinese,' so I wasn't expecting you to understand me—let alone answer me."

Rose was drowsy, but this new information roused her a bit.

"Chan was my maiden name," she explained, "and I must've been confused when I was brought in—I mean, to be speaking Chinese! I don't even speak it that well."

"Well enough to make the admitting nurse think that you were from the old country, so to speak," the nurse said brightly. "As for the name, would you mind telling me what I should put on all the paperwork that we must keep up with?"

"Winterslip, Rose Winterslip," Rose replied, spelling the last name, "and I'd like to go home, please."

"Now, then, that's all right, you rest and don't trouble yourself," the woman said kindly, brandishing a thermometer. "Just hold this under your tongue for a bit and try not to talk.

"Doctor says you're probably just dehydrated. Nothing serious—you just need fluids and rest. Hold that still for just a minute or two more, and then you can tell me whatever else is on your mind." She smiled.

"As if I didn't know! And you needn't worry about that, dearie—Mrs. Winterslip. Doctor says your baby isn't quite ready to join us, but everything looks fine, just fine."

Rose was relieved. She lay still and tried to collect her thoughts, but the last several hours were a blur.

"There we are—normal, just as I expected," the white-capped attendant said triumphantly, holding the thermometer up to the light. She made some notes on the chart. "Now, where were we—anything else I can tell you for the present?"

"My husband—he brought me here—where—"

"Any family member would be waiting downstairs for you," the nurse reassured her. "But you won't be able to see anyone right now because Doctor gave you a mild sedative so that you can get some rest. That's the best thing for you and the baby.

"I'll leave you in peace for the time being," the nurse concluded. "Time to update my records as to your proper last name and so on, but your job is to go to sleep! Best thing for you and the baby," she repeated in a firm voice, "is to get some rest."

"I guess I must've been a bit confused earlier," Rose repeated dreamily. "One more thing—"

"Yes?"

"How's Jane?" She gestured sleepily in the direction of the other bed.

"Jane?" The nurse replied in a baffled tone. "Is that a friend of yours?"

"No, no—we just met, Jane and I," Rose struggled to lift her head, turning toward the bed next to hers.

It wasn't there.

"You've been having a dream, dearie," the nurse said sympathetically. "Unless you met Jane on your way to the hospital—"

"She was right here," Rose insisted, "in the next bed. We spoke, I introduced myself. The chart on the side of her bed said her name was 'Jane Doe.' "

The nurse's baffled expression dissolved into gentle laughter.

"My goodness, what a dream you've been having! Not every patient of mine falls asleep and fancies herself encountering 'Jane Doe.' " She patted Rose's hand. "Not a terribly original name for a dream woman."

"But it wasn't a dream," Rose murmured. "Jane was in the bed next to mine, and we spoke."

"Now, now—you can see for yourself that yours is the only bed in the room. Sometimes patients have the strangest dreams when they're sedated, but it's nothing for you to worry yourself about."

"Please tell my husband—my mother—"

The woman patted Rose's hand again reassuringly.

"I'll tell them, dearie, I'll tell them. You just close your eyes and in a few hours you'll feel much better."

Rose drifted off. The nurse walked quietly from the room, closing the door behind her, and returned to her station where the paperwork was unending.

She transferred vital statistics from the errant medical chart, which she discarded, to a new one with the patient's correct name. And she updated the patient census, crossing out "Chan, Rose" and adding "Winterslip, Rose."

In the wastebasket lay a crumpled sheet that read "Rose Chan." In one corner of the discarded record was a small circular mark—the mark Rose was sure she had seen on Jane Doe's chart.

In a first-floor hospital waiting room Henry Chan tried to reassure his mother while John Quincy Winterslip approached a stern-looking nurse reigning over the reception desk.

"Excuse me, I'd like to—"

"One moment, sir," the personage cut in. She was writing rapidly on the topmost form stacked on a clipboard. "I'll be with you presently."

John Quincy waited patiently, observing the woman at work. She was about forty, perhaps a little younger, and her name tag read, "Hilda Brunn, Registered Nurse."

Since Miss Brunn wore no wedding ring, Winterslip idly speculated that her parents must have been devoted to Wagner's Ring Cycle—and that they were also, perhaps, possessed of a puckish sense of humor. *It must have been shattering for her when the class roll was called in last-name-first order*, he mused.

In appearance "Brunn, Hilda" (as John Quincy now thought of her) was less formidable than her archetypal namesake. Short in stature, she had a sharp chin, pursed lips and small eyes crowned by a furrowed brow. A wisp of light-brown hair fleeing from the front edge of her white cap danced to and fro as she nodded in time with her vigorous penmanship.

The seconds dragged on, and John Quincy's patience waned with each tick of his wrist-watch. After what seemed an interminable delay Nurse Brunn completed the administrative task, put down her pen and directed an inquiring look at the father-to-be.

"Yes? How can I help you?"

"My wife—her name is Rose Winterslip—I drove her here about forty-five minutes ago. They said—"

"What was the nature of your wife's medical complaint?"

"She's expecting. The doctor said it would be soon, and this morning she began to have pains, sharp pains—"

"Ah—she would be in the maternity wing, then." The severity of the nurse's expression decreased slightly. "Let me check the sheet from upstairs."

Setting aside the clipboard in front of her, she reached for a second one which hung from a hook next to her desk.

The nurse frowned at the clipboard's top sheet, then looked up and transferred the frown to John Quincy.

"You said the name is 'Winterslip'—and the first name is?"

"Rose. Rose Winterslip," John Quincy emphasized, trying to control his growing irritation.

"Hmm. I don't see anything here . . . are you sure that—"

"Yes, quite sure. As I said, we arrived less than an hour ago. Maybe your list hasn't been updated?"

"Oh, no, this was brought down from the ward a short while ago so it's quite current." The frown wavered. After returning to the clipboard, Nurse Brunn reached for the phone.

"Just a moment while I call the admitting office. They should be able to tell us if she's a patient in a department other than maternity."

John Quincy was confused.

"But why wouldn't she be—"

"In maternity?" Brunn dialed an internal number and waited. "Sometimes the admitting physician in a case like this will decide the mother-to-be would benefit from treatment other than—that is to say, a woman might not be ready for the maternity ward.

"Hmm. No answer." She cradled the receiver and sighed. "Why don't you just have a seat, Mr. Winterslip, and I'll try again shortly. There's really no cause for concern." The frown was now almost a smile. "We seldom lose a patient in this hospital."

"Thanks, that's very . . . reassuring," said John Quincy, who was anything but reassured. "You've been very helpful."

Brunn, Hilda, Registered Nurse, nodded dismissively.

John Quincy Winterslip lit a cigarette and walked slowly toward his in-laws. Henry was flipping through a ten-year-old issue of *West Coast Life* magazine and his mother, on the edge of her seat, looked up eagerly.

"How is Rose, please? We can see her now?" As it often did, Mrs. Chan's questioning tone indicated something between a request and a command. Henry turned his gaze toward his brother-in-law inquiringly. Winterslip addressed them both.

"There's been a slight mix-up in the hospital records—nothing to worry about. I'm going to go upstairs and straighten it out."

Henry's mother started to rise, but John Quincy shook his head.

"I think it would be better if you both go home, and I'll call you as soon as I find out more." Calmly, respectfully, he interrupted his mother-in-law's objections: "I understand that we'd all like to be here, but it may be some time—and you'll be more comfortable at home.

"And please," he added, in a quiet aside to Henry, "look after your mother, all right?"

Henry nodded and patted his mother on the shoulder. Outnumbered, she agreed to follow John Quincy's advice.

"But you will call soon, yes?" Mama Chan demanded. "Little Rose will need her mama."

John Quincy assured his mother-in-law that any news would be relayed at once, and Henry gently took the arm of the family matriarch and guided her toward the exit.

Consulting a building directory on the wall John Quincy discarded his cigarette in a standing ashtray. He walked quickly to the elevator and stood in front of its closed door for a moment, eyeing the floor indicator impatiently before heading for the nearest stairwell.

The maternity department was on the third floor, according to the directory. Taking the stairs two at a time Winterslip arrived slightly out of breath and made his way to what appeared to be a receiving desk or nurse's station.

No one was in evidence so John Quincy made use of a small service bell. Just then a white-uniformed woman exited the elevator and approached.

"May I help you?" The nurse posed the question as she took her place behind the receiving desk.

"Yes, I hope so," Winterslip replied, reminding himself to remain calm. "I'm looking for my wife. I brought her to the hospital some time ago, and downstairs they had no record of her, so—"

"You came up here to see for yourself," the nurse put in. "Of course. Many expectant fathers do that very thing. I'm guessing this is your first time?"

John Quincy nodded.

"And what's your wife's full name, please?"

Winterslip provided the particulars, and the nurse turned from page to page in her record-book.

"Oh, yes! The admitting office called just a few minutes ago to correct an error. Your wife's name was mistakenly entered as Rose Chan—her maiden name?"

John Quincy nodded.

"I gather that she was admitted in some haste," the nurse rattled on. "Sometimes errors happen with incoming patients in distress. Here we are, "Winterslip, Rose"—so that makes you Mr. Winterslip, yes?—your wife is in room 311. She may be sleeping, but you're welcome to check."

She pointed down the long corridor.

"It's about half-way down the hall, past the passenger elevator and the stairwell. If you come to the freight elevator you'll know you've gone too far. Remember, number three-one-one."

Thanking the nurse, John Quincy set off in the indicated direction, dodging the occasional white-garbed staff member and navigating around gurneys on which patients were either in transit or parked temporarily against the corridor wall.

The expectant father-to-be had successfully avoided more than one collision with hospital personnel and their charges when he realized that he was passing a large set of elevator doors marked "Freight Only."

As he read the sign he turned around to retrace his steps and bumped into one of the motionless wheeled stretchers against the wall. The occupant, covered by a sheet up to her chin, reminded him of Rose at first glance. She blinked and slowly looked up at John Quincy.

"So sorry—I ran into your—please excuse me," Winterslip stammered. "Hope I didn't disturb you."

The woman's eyes opened wide, and her hand shot out from beneath the white sheet to grasp Winterslip's arm. Startled, he looked at the hand gripping him and noticed what looked like an inkstain on the left wrist, a half-black circular mark with two dots.

"Please—" The woman's voice trailed off into what sounded like gibberish to Winterslip's untutored ear, syllables arriving in a jumble that was repeated more than once.

With a clang the freight elevator doors opened to reveal a broad-shouldered, white-gowned and masked orderly. Nodding to Winterslip, he took charge of the parked gurney.

"Ah, there you are, Jane! They've sent me to take you on a nice trip downstairs, so just close your eyes and we'll be on our way."

As the white-coated man pushed the gurney into the elevator and pressed a button the woman he called Jane continued to mumble the string of sounds, apparently addressing them to the uncomprehending John Quincy until the doors closed.

Retracing his steps he located room 311. The door was ajar and the room was dimly lit, but he could see well enough to recognize the sole occupant. Rose woke with a start as John Quincy approached her bed.

"Thank heaven you're here," she murmured drowsily. "I want to report a missing roommate."

Rose recounted her brief conversation with the woman, who according to the nurse didn't exist, and told her husband about the circular mark on her chart. John Quincy frowned.

"A woman here, then not here," he said. "I think I know where she went."

He quickly summarized his encounter down the hall. "As for the mark on her wrist, it sounds quite a lot like the little circle you describe on your ex-roommate's chart," John Quincy mused. "I'd lay odds it was she I encountered briefly down the hall—the attendant called her Jane."

Rose grimaced. A certain discomfort had reminded her why she was paying a visit to the maternity ward.

"Her chart," she said, taking a deep breath and exhaling slowly, "it said Jane Doe. "But why the markings? Some new hospital record-keeping method?"

"No-o-o . . ." John Quincy said slowly. "I don't think so. From the little I could see of the one on Jane's wrist, it looked like something—something I've seen in Boston. To be more precise, in the old home city's Chinatown district."

"I wish I had seen her chart more closely," Rose said ruefully, "but it was near the foot of her bed—and I was barely awake."

Her eyes flashed in indignation.

"But why did the nurse pretend Jane Doe was never here?" Rose demanded. "What's going on?"

"Something peculiar is going on here, that's what," John Quincy declared.

Chapter Seven

HOURS OF DARKNESS

Pearl City Peninsula took on a golden hue in the late afternoon, and few clouds interfered with the setting sun's rays. Encouraged by a cool breeze from the northeast, the fronds of a coconut palm near the pier seemed to wave goodbye to some two dozen people waiting to board a sea plane.

Only a few years ago air travel from Hawaii to and from points east and west was only for the adventurous, those seeking to make history and set records. Now, for a substantial price, a traveler in need of greater speed than a Matson liner's four-day cruising time could fly from Honolulu to San Francisco in little more than eighteen hours.

"Don't worry about the ticket," the Chief had told Charlie Chan, whose official frugality was well known to his colleagues. "I'm sure that enough of your time will be devoted to business that the department can spare a few hundred dollars for a one-way fare.

Mind you," he had added hastily, "take the slow way home! You'll probably need a few days to relax, and I've heard that it's easier to sleep on a Matson liner than on one of those flying boats."

As the line of boarding passengers moved toward the cabin door Chan contemplated the great silver craft with some trepidation. Trips by ship, rail, automobile—to these he had become accustomed, but to cross the ocean far above it while traveling at an unimaginable speed? With a sigh he resigned himself to this new experience.

"Man is but a leaf that bobs in current of the fates," Charlie Chan was fond of saying, acknowledging that even his comings and goings sometimes attracted the attention of the gods. They seemed to arrange events in his vicinity that challenged and fulfilled his professional aspirations—so he had no qualms about his maiden flight.

"*If same gods decide both detective's career and life span,*" he thought wryly, "*then they can persuade flying ship to arrive safely at its appointed destination.*"

Making his way aboard Chan exchanged greetings with welcoming crew members, one of whom took charge of the detective's luggage, and made his way into the main passenger cabin. As was his habit when traveling he examined individual passengers and crew with a seemingly cursory gaze.

Starting with the steward who had taken charge of his luggage, Chan's survey included an elderly gentleman traveling alone; the talkative man and woman (husband and wife?) seated together; a plump gray-haired woman near them, also traveling alone; two men in suits (business associates?) conversing in low tones; two nuns, further back; and a middle-aged man in Western business attire. Even the steward who fulfilled his order for an "orange-juice drink" was subjected to Chan's scrutiny.

All those the detective observed, even briefly, unknowingly revealed something of themselves to him. Whatever insights and deductions resulted were stored away for possible future use. At the very least the exercise was useful for one whose natural deductive abilities and ever-present instincts never dulled, a policeman whose remarkable memory for faces and other personal details often astounded his colleagues.

As the plane became airborne and evening gradually turned into night, Chan's thoughts turned from his fellow passengers to family and the much-anticipated event that awaited him in

San Francisco. Lulled by the low, rumbling hum of the engines he reclined the couch-like seat and closed his eyes for what he hoped would be a restful night.

Thousands of feet above the dark waters of the Pacific the Clipper droned northeastward through the night. Some passengers occupied semi-private sleeping berths like those on a train; others, like Chan, preferred to sleep in their reclining seats.

Suddenly the detective awakened.

In the split second it took to recall his surroundings he imagined himself on the deckchair of an ocean liner bound for the mainland. Then the murmuring of the aircraft's engines reminded him that the ocean was far below.

Something had awakened him—what, he could not tell—but all was quiet now, and he felt as rested as if he had been asleep for hours. Consulting his wrist-watch, a gift from daughter Rose years ago, he realized that little more than an hour had passed since he closed his eyes.

Fully awake he lay quietly and returned his thoughts to his wife, Rose, son-in-law John Quincy and son Henry. Perhaps the Chief was right and he would arrive in time to be present for the arrival of this first grandchild, but Chan was content to let events take their course. It was enough that he would see the new arrival and celebrate the occasion with family.

Even though sleep had fled, the detective remained motionless in consideration of the other passengers. He assumed that they were all sleeping soundly judging from the deep, steady breathing close at hand and a faint, far-off snoring coming from the rear of the compartment.

Chan's pleasant family ruminations continued for a minute or more, complemented by the engines' muffled purring.

One word, then another, spoken in muted tones just above a whisper, interrupted the detective's thoughts. Always respectful of others' privacy he was conscious of the exchanges but tried to ignore them—at first.

Until the words and their context could no longer be ignored.

"Awake?"

"Yes."

"Too much risk, too dangerous."

"You're imagining things."

"No. Customs and police—"

"Hush!"

"I'm afraid of—"

The snorer in the back of the compartment awakened with a thunderous snort that disturbed more than a few of the other passengers. The conversation Chan had happened to overhear came to an abrupt end.

The detective was intrigued. The words he had just heard were capable of multiple interpretations, he thought—some benign, others less so. The positioning of the passengers in fairly close proximity, in total darkness, combined with the low, persistent background noise of the aircraft, made it impossible for him to pinpoint the source of the two whisperers.

With hours of darkness to go he could not even mingle casually with other passengers to gauge which two had carried on the subdued conversation and might be involved in—in what, exactly? Smuggling of some kind, contraband, prohibited items small enough to be concealed in personal baggage? Something relatively harmless—or a more serious crime?

Chan resolved to continue his vigil, at least for several minutes, in hopes that he might overhear an additional conversation that would allow him to better place the speakers. Daylight and breakfast could then afford an opportunity to view fellow passengers, even converse with them in hopes of recognizing the voices of the two. The darkness was such that he could only see the luminous numbers and hands of his wrist-watch so he calculated that dawn would not break for some time still.

A flash of impatience clouded his thoughts as he chafed at the delay, but the cloud was dispersed as the words of Kong Fu Tse came to mind: "*Want of forbearance in small matters confounds great plans.*"

True, Chan thought wryly, *except that in the present case I do not know whether these are "small matters" or if "great plans" even exist.*

He closed his eyes, listened to the hum of the engines and waited for the new day.

Chapter Eight

BREAKFAST ON THE CLIPPER

On a quiet San Francisco street where several Victorian houses had survived the earthquake and fire years ago the Homeplace Orphanage held forth in a rambling Gothic pile once home to a family called Lande.

A small institution in a large house, Homeplace turned a prosperous face to the outside world, but its inner appearances told a different story. Once elegant decor had given way to austere furnishings, faded wallpaper and peeling paint. What was once a high-ceilinged drawing room now featured a dozen or more battered school desks arranged in rows. Several second-floor bedroom walls had been knocked down to create a dormitory with two dozen beds and cots lined up in barracks fashion.

The room across the hall from the group sleeping quarters had retained much of its original style, including an old four-poster bed with canopy and curtains and a few other items of furniture. The only recent additions were a small corner desk with matching chair, and a bench big enough for up to two guests.

Virginia Lande was fond of the room. She had spent much of her childhood in it, and now it served as her office and general headquarters. As matron of Homeplace, she ran and resided in the orphanage, ably assisted by live-in assistant Gladys Tembleton and a small and ever-changing roster of part-time workers.

An only daughter of Norwegian immigrants, Lande had never married. Although childless, she treated the youngsters in the care of Homeplace Orphanage as her own.

Her matronly appearance agreed with her chosen profession. Long past forty, she was stout and red-faced, hands roughened by daily work, hair just beginning to gray gathered in a bun. She favored the common woman's workaday fashion from a previous generation, especially drab full-length dresses.

The Homeplace census varied, but the house could accommodate no more than twenty candidates for adoption. While most of what Lande referred to as "the family" were no younger than four and no older than fourteen, infants were placed through the home under certain circumstances, usually just one at a time.

The children, especially the younger ones, came and went frequently; Lande said the city was fortunate to have so many childless couples willing to adopt. Staff turnover also contributed to the number of new faces and nearly constant changes in routine.

Her charges thought of her less as a mother and more as a maiden aunt. Even when disciplining the errant she endeared herself to them with a sorrowful look through steel-rimmed spectacles . . . as though she felt the children's waywardness, their pain, as her own.

It was well after midday, and Lande was navigating some of the constant changes in expectation that arose both outside the small institution and within it. Homeplace's current residents were at their studies in the converted classroom so the household was relatively quiet.

Until a sudden interruption ended Lande's peaceful interlude.

"I'm sure I don't know what to do about it, ma'am," wailed Gladys. "Where we're going to find the room and all—"

Virginia Lande replaced the telephone receiver to its cradle and turned from her desk to face this noisy interruption to her day's work.

"Why, Gladys! Whatever is the matter now? I thought we had settled things quite nicely."

"Yes, ma'am, things was settled fine, but we've been told to expect two new infant arrivals, and I don't see where we're going to put them since, well, you know—we're really up to our ears in older children already, if you'll pardon the expression."

The pale-faced girl in her late teens was that rare case—a Homeplace orphan who had never left the establishment. Gladys had grown into a staff position, a kind of maid-of-all-work. She tended to get "all worked up" as Lande had said on more than one occasion, and the long speech had left poor Gladys out of breath.

"Now, now, you needn't worry yourself," the matron replied soothingly. "You know very well that these things are temporary. You mustn't get so excited."

"Yes, but—"

"In fact I've just learned that we'll only be taking on one infant and only for a few days. I'm sure you'll make everyone feel at home, and we'll all adjust."

"It's just that I don't—"

Virginia Lande stood and grasped Gladys's hands.

"My dear girl," she said kindly. "We make these sacrifices for the children, for their future wellbeing. Surely occasional inconveniences such as these are worth it, aren't they?"

The young woman nodded tearfully.

"I'll certainly do my best, ma'am." She drew a handkerchief from an apron pocket and wiped her eyes. Lande eyed her thoughtfully.

"I know you will." The matron smiled. "Now, then. Make sure the children don't see any tears. Most of them have had enough unhappiness already."

Gladys blew her nose affirmatively.

"Thank you, ma'am. I'll see to things right away."

The faithful assistant departed, and Virginia Lande sighed.

'Perfect faith is nowhere to be found,' she thought. *How true.*

Charlie Chan customarily rose with the dawn if not before it, and he was awake and ready for breakfast before most of the other passengers began to stir. The plane's design allowed for the main passenger cabin to serve as a dining room, and a white-jacketed steward deftly transformed the furnishings into three booths, each with white tablecloth and place settings for four.

The detective found himself seated with three of the fellow passengers he had observed earlier, the pair of nuns and the man Chan had mentally categorized as a Japanese businessman or government official. Introductions were exchanged as the steward brought coffee and orange juice.

One of the two nuns opened the proceedings.

"Good morning! I'm Sister Clarice, and this is my associate, Sister Margareta."

Both women were dressed in the traditional garb of a Roman Catholic religious, with mostly black habits and headpieces revealing only their faces and hands. Chan noted the sharp contrast between the two: He perceived with silent amusement that the speaker's pale complexion, apparently aided by some cosmetic, was almost as white as the guimpe draped around her neck, shoulders and chest. Her companion's darker-hued face was not many shades lighter than the black habits that covered the two from head to foot.

"Happy to make the acquaintance of two daughters of Our Lady of Troubled Pilgrims Sacred Order," Chan half-rose from the confines of the breakfast booth and bowed. "I am Charlie Chan of Honolulu. Your works are well known in the islands and beyond."

"Why, Mr. Chan, how kind of you!" Sister Clarice exclaimed. "May I ask how you knew that we were of the Sacred Order?"

Chan smiled.

"Catholic sisters who take monastic vows wear clothing particular to their order—each team has different uniform, as my cousin Willy Chan says of baseball players. The habits, veils and wimples of the Sacred Order members differ from those of other groups of holy women. I have encountered members of your order in Honolulu schools, in hospitals and other places."

"Quite true, and very astute, Mr. Chan," the nun beamed, thin lips parting to reveal gleaming teeth. "But I'm forgetting my manners in neglecting the other member of our party, Mr. — ?"

Sister Clarice gestured toward the fourth passenger at their table, who stood and bowed in response.

"Takahashi. Kyoshi Takahashi." Resuming his seat, he smiled and added. "I have . . . little English."

"That's perfectly all right, Mr. Takahashi," Sister Clarice uttered the name carefully, succeeding in reproducing most of it. "You are in good company in that regard, as Sister Margareta" — she gestured toward her companion, who smiled and nodded — "is lately arrived from our African mission, and she really speaks no English at all."

"Good." Sister Margareta offered, nodding repeatedly at the two men. "Day," she said uncertainly, pausing before delivering a final word: "All."

"That's right, Sister—'Good day, all,'" Sister Clarice said encouragingly. "Splendid! Your English is coming along quite well."

The steward returned with a heavily laden tray and presented breakfast with a flourish.

"Ladies and gentlemen, this morning we offer you chilled cantaloupe, scrambled eggs with diced bacon and a homemade breakfast pastry. Please enjoy, and let me know if you require anything else."

Having delivered breakfast and the accompanying remarks he smiled and departed.

"Well! Isn't this delightful!" Sister Clarice daintily took a bite of the egg entrée as her compatriot sampled the pastry. Mr. Takahashi followed suit, and Chan tasted a slice of cantaloupe. It was remarkably fresh, and he marveled at the efficiency of an airline that could organize the onboarding of locally grown fruits as well as passengers and their baggage.

"Miracles of science continue to astonish as they advance daily life beyond all expectations," the detective remarked. "Not many years ago I experienced the marvel of ocean travel from home islands to mainland for the first time. Wonders of big ship were equally amazing to me then as present reality of eating breakfast while flying high above the ocean is now."

The eggs "with diced bacon" apparently were delicious; Sister Clarice swallowed a mouthful and dabbed her lips with a cloth napkin before replying.

"How true, Mr. Chan! So many wonderful things undreamt of in our youth—certainly in *my* childhood—are becoming commonplace," she declared. "Although I must say that this 'flying meal,' if one may call it that, cannot compare to the variety of foods available to passengers on the ocean liners you mentioned."

Chan nodded in agreement. "I have found so much food on occasions of sea travel too agreeable, adding to my already substantial girth," he said ruefully. "But you and companion sister—you have traveled frequently on ocean voyages, perhaps between Hawaii and mainland?"

The fork on its way to more eggs paused.

"Oh, my goodness—no, indeed," the nun said hastily, her thin eyebrows arching alarmingly. "I didn't mean to imply that I—we certainly haven't traveled widely. In fact," she added, "our vow of poverty would make such a thing impossible. In fact, this flight is unusual for members of our order. It was made possible by a generous donor."

"Generosity to those in need—the idea blossoms in all religions like flowers in spring," Chan remarked. "Noble benefactor provided means of swift transportation for sisters on mission of mercy?"

"That's it exactly, Mr. Chan, you describe it very well." Sister Clarice put down her fork and took a sip of coffee. The table's other two occupants were doing justice to their scrambled eggs, their interest in the conversation apparently limited by the language barrier.

"You probably are aware that the sisters have worked for many years to help find homes for orphaned children on the islands," the nun explained. "It's been part of the order's work since our founders arrived there many years ago."

"I have been aware of your order and others for a long time—have seen many nuns on the islands active in education and work with young people," Chan remarked. "My own offspring sampled good works of the sisters during long-ago summer programs for youth.

Sad to report," the detective said with a grin, "that heathen Chan children remain unconverted to Roman faith—while fond of music, they complained of too much kneeling every day and fasting on Fridays. The young," he observed, "often must satisfy physical appetite before addressing spiritual hunger."

Both nuns nodded and smiled.

"Also must report that I remain unconverted," Chan continued, "but have great admiration for your dedication, especially to children most in need."

Sister Clarice laughed quietly and brought her hands together briefly in a prayerful gesture.

"Ah, Mr. Chan, I know that you are only jesting—'kidding me along,' as our children would put it—about 'heathens.' Such an unpleasant and outdated word! No, we prefer to serve the people of the islands directly through good works that you so kindly mentioned. Above all, we try to teach by example."

Chan nodded. "Practical application of religious devotion is capable of great things, whichever particular holy philosophy is followed. Religion, like modern roadways, offers many paths that lead to the same destination."

"So true! Of course we know that *our* particular path is the right one," the nun said matter-of-factly. "However, in answer to your question: Through our benefactor we have become aware of the potential for placing children for adoption on the mainland. Sister Margareta and I are going to visit one of the San Francisco orphanages that the order has been corresponding with."

She nodded encouragingly at the other nun, who smiled in return.

"We're what you might call a scouting party," Sister Clarice explained. "We shall investigate the possibilities, meet with some of the interested parties and return and report our findings to Mother Superior.

"You see," she continued, "ensuring that our work persists requires a great deal of outreach—and we have high hopes that this effort will bear fruit."

The other nun nodded emphatically and retrieved a few more words from her limited stock of English.

"Children . . . babies," she emphasized each word, speaking slowly, "uh . . . place-home." The last two words came out as one, and Sister Margareta smiled triumphantly and nodded enthusiastically.

"Very good indeed, Sister," Sister Clarice said encouragingly. "Building your vocabulary one word at a time is a splendid way to master a new language.

"And Sister Margareta has expressed the heart of our mission in far fewer words than I have," the nun acknowledged. "We are dedicated to the proposition that these children—sometimes even infants—deserve to be placed in a loving home."

Chan nodded.

"Do sisters' plans include much activity?" he inquired politely. "Many visits to orphanages and other institutions?"

"Oh, dear me, no—our time is so limited that we will only be able to fulfill the engagement with the institution specified by our donor," Sister Clarice said, her face expressing to Chan's watchful eyes a moment of . . . regret? Annoyance? The detective wondered.

"Sadly, there just isn't time, even though I'm sure there are many other worthy organizations we might consider. Perhaps in the future . . . " She paused as though a stray thought had occurred.

"Have you been to San Francisco before, Mr. Chan?" the nun continued. "Your family name—"

"Indeed, as one who shares ancient name with many immigrants on mainland I have visited famous city several times," Chan cut in, hoping to forestall a discussion of his professional history. "Family members reside there, and I go to join my wife for vacation time with daughter and son-in-law."

"How nice!" Sister Clarice beamed. With that, her stream of conversation ceased to flow—at least temporarily. Chan's gaze rested thoughtfully for a moment on the two nuns before his eyes met briefly with those of the Japanese.

Mr. Takahashi returned the detective's look with one of bland indifference.

Some hours had elapsed since breakfast aboard the huge airplane, and the passengers had returned to their separate pursuits: reading, napping, quiet conversation. Charlie Chan divided his thoughts between his coming reunion with family and his last conversation with the Chief.

The detective sensed that there might be more to the request from his old friend Tom Flannery than the Chief's simple summary. Chan resolved to give the matter his full attention during these idle hours of air travel. Even now, he was intrigued by certain aspects of his first Clipper trip.

The time passed quickly for him, and a change in the humming engine noise suggested that the flight was coming to an end.

In the afternoon light the detective trained his eyes on what he could see of the coastline ahead. Approaching Alameda, the great flying boat turned and Chan glimpsed Coit Tower, one of the few city landmarks he could readily identify from this vantage point.

"It seems as though we'll be landing shortly," Sister Clarice called from her nearby seat. "I have so enjoyed meeting you, Mr. Chan."

The detective bowed slightly from his seat. "I am happy to have made the acquaintance of you and your colleague in holy work." Sister Margareta returned Chan's bow with a nod and a smile.

"Perhaps we'll meet again—San Francisco in many ways is a small city," Sister Clarice continued, her voice competing with the growing drone of the Clipper's four engines.

Chan smiled.

"Who can say? According to old Chinese proverb, two separated even by thousands of miles will meet again—if the fates decree it."

Chapter Nine

"HELP—SAVE MY LIFE"

A Pan American Clipper's arrival at Benton Field was not attended by as much fanfare now as it would have been just a few years before, when regular Pacific flights were inaugurated. Still, disembarking passengers were greeted by family and friends, and Charlie Chan saw a familiar face in the small crowd.

"Dad! It's great to see you on the ground—all in one piece, too!" Henry Chan shouted over the noise of the just-arrived Clipper and the hustle and bustle of the landing field. "How does it feel to be an aeronaut?"

The elder Chan grimaced, securing his hat against a brisk wind with one hand and patting his substantial midriff with the other.

"My past discomfort during ocean voyages is now a fond memory compared to effects of flying boat on middle-aged man's inner workings," he lamented. "Even more than butter-flies in stomach, I have sensation like insect on arrow shot to distant target."

Henry laughed as the two collected the detective's luggage and made their way toward John Quincy's waiting car parked near the pier.

After stowing the luggage in the sedan's trunk, Henry got behind the wheel and turned to his front-seat passenger.

"So, where do you want to go first?"

Chan looked inquiringly at his son.

"To answer your question, I must ask one: Where are Rose and your mother? And John Quincy?"

Henry lit a cigarette and started the engine, easing the automobile into the stream of motorized and pedestrian traffic typical of the district.

" 'Thereby hangs a tale,' as a famous Englishman once put it," Henry replied, steering the sedan confidently, if a bit too quickly for his father's taste. "Let me acquaint you with all that has occurred within the last forty-eight hours or so."

The younger Chan began with a summary of his time on the *Monterey* and the people he had encountered: assistant steward Notley, and his desire for a private conversation; the "Jack Sprat and wife" Mr. and Mrs. Perkins, and the latter's interest in Charlie Chan; and Notley's failure to show up at Calico Jim's.

Henry's recital also included the briefing he had received from John Quincy. The monologue continued until Chan suggested they find a telephone before going further toward either home or hospital.

"Good idea! There's a booth on that corner," Henry exclaimed, braking suddenly and pulling the car abreast of the curb. "I'll be back as soon as I contribute a nickel toward the cost of the Telephone Building." He laughed at his father's look of puzzlement and explained. "Pacific Telephone and Telegraph—several years ago they put up the tallest building in the city. Rose told me she and John Quincy kid each other every time they pick up the phone that they're helping pay the mortgage for it."

Henry was quick about it. In a very few minutes he returned.

"We're off to the hospital," he announced excitedly. "I spoke to John Quincy, and he said it won't be long now!"

The maternity ward waiting room provided few amenities for those anxiously anticipating new arrivals. As though the hospital knew that its visitors would stand and pace rather than sit and relax, the room's furnishings were long on functionality and short on comfort.

The chairs in rows and even a lone settee appeared more sturdy than inviting, and a series of Currier and Ives prints depicting happy children barely relieved the monotony of walls painted in shades of institutional green and gray.

When its occupancy was strained by circumstances the waiting room's smoke-filled atmosphere gave it the feeling of a gambling parlor, albeit one in which the prevailing wager consisted of a mere coin flip: boy or girl.

Charlie and Henry Chan spied Chan Chun Shee and John Quincy, both pacing. Winterslip was smoking as he strode back and forth, and near collisions among the Chan family contingent and a half-dozen or so other pacers provided an occasional break in the tension.

After the family patriarch was greeted by his wife and son-in-law with all due affection, John Quincy pulled Chan aside for a quiet talk.

"Henry has already described recent events in some detail," Chan replied to Winterslip's opening volley of information. "Perhaps you have additional items of interest to combine with eldest son's list?"

John Quincy summarized what he had encountered or observed in Henry's absence, with Chan putting in an occasional question or comment.

"I don't mean to make a mystery where there is none," John Quincy concluded, "and I probably would have dismissed the confusion over Rose's whereabouts as an administrative error—"

"If not for strange encounter with woman who had mark on wrist," Chan put in. "Also, your uneasiness grows at a time when family event already produces anxiety, so—"

"So maybe the whole thing is a mare's nest?" Winterslip concluded with a trace of chagrin in his voice. "I admit that detection is not my area of expertise, but when that woman grabbed my arm and said, well, whatever it was that she said—with such fear in her voice—"

"Please pardon my rude interruptions," Chan cut in, "but you have said woman appeared Asian—maybe Chinese? If so, maybe urgent sounds she made were meaningless to you because she spoke in native tongue."

"Rose has been teaching me a few words and phrases right along," John Quincy acknowledged, "but I didn't recognize what that woman said at all." He paused as though he had just thought of something. "Maybe she was sedated, maybe the drugs were slurring her words."

"Please, make effort to reproduce sounds as you recall them," Chan urged.

John Quincy closed his eyes and concentrated.

"I thought at first she was just babbling, but then I realized she was repeating the same sounds, over and over again," Winterslip murmured. "Now that I think back on it, I'm pretty sure that she was saying three things, three syllables, and then repeating them."

"What three sounds, please?" Chan said encouragingly.

"The first one was something like 'cow,' I'm pretty sure," Winterslip opened his eyes and grinned at his father-in-law. "That's what first got me thinking that she was just babbling, talking about a cow didn't make any sense to me."

Chan frowned.

"Other two syllables?"

"The second one was 'ming,' like the pottery," Winterslip said brightly.

" 'Ming,' like great imperial dynasty of China," Chan amended with a sigh. "Also known for things other than fine ceramics.

"Third sound you heard, please?"

"The last one was easy," John Quincy said with certainty. "It ran together with the other two, and it was just 'ah.' So she said—whispered, really—'cow ming ah,' and then repeated it."

Chan's expression darkened.

"Picture of suspicion begins to come into better focus," he said. "You say woman called Jane had mark on wrist and similar mark was seen by Rose on roommate Jane's medical chart. Small circle you describe seeing on woman must have been crude rendering of 'yin-yang'."

"What does it mean?" the younger man queried.

"Yin-Yang is a very old Chinese symbol with many meanings. Balance of all things—dark and light, male and female, and so on— can bring about harmony. Its meaning here is unclear, but what purpose does it serve?" Chan replied.

"Woman Jane and daughter Rose—similar in appearance, placed in same room, but Jane is marked in strange manner and removed from room while Rose remains. Why?

"An important question, but not as vital as the words that you heard," the detective continued. "This unfortunate woman feared for her life. Her words were desperate plea for help, spoken in Cantonese."

Winterslip looked alarmed.

"What was the urgent message? What was she trying to say?"

"What you heard as 'cow ming ah' was surely *gau meng ah*," Chan replied gravely. "Translation from Cantonese is usually, 'Help, save me.'"

He paused.

"Sometimes translation is 'Help—save my life.'"

"Mr. Winterslip?"

John Quincy had not yet absorbed Chan's revelatory translation when their conversation was interrupted by a white-gowned physician. It was none other than Dr. Klindleman, with Mrs. Chan and Henry in his wake.

"Good news," Dr. K. beamed from beneath his white cap, a surgical mask dangling around his neck. "It's a girl. A fine, healthy baby girl. Congratulations!"

The waiting room tension vanished for the Chans as they exchanged hugs and handshakes, and the new grandmother shed a few tears of celebration. The other pacers in the room looked on with interest, hoping that their relief would soon arrive. John Quincy distributed cigars to both of the Chan men and the doctor.

"Please, may we see daughter Rose?" Mrs. Chan said timidly. "And new granddaughter, too?"

"I think a few minutes will do no harm," Dr. K. replied. "Rose is awake, but she's going to need her rest. So, no long visits at this stage."

"And granddaughter?" Chan Chun Shee persisted.

"In a short while you'll be able to see the little one in the nursery with all the other recent arrivals," Dr. K. assured her. "Just through the glass window for now. You see, we have to maintain a germ-free environment for newborns as much as possible.

"Why don't all of you follow me, and you can say hello to the new mother?"

The Chans enjoyed a joyous few minutes with a smiling but pale Rose, and a nurse soon arrived to escort them down the hall to the nursery viewing area. A half-dozen infants lay in individual bassinets, a card at the foot of each denoting last name and date of arrival. As they scanned the six tiny occupants through the glass the Chans were rewarded by the arrival of a seventh as a nurse wheeled a bassinet into the room, its card proclaiming, "Baby Girl Winterslip."

Father and grandparents fixed their attention on the little cherub, whose only response was the partial insertion of a fist into her mouth. This and other small movements were greeted by the three with glee as they debated the great question of family resemblance and the associated issues of hair (there was quite a bit of it, of uncertain hue) and eye color.

Leaving the three to their through-the-glass encounter with the newest family member Henry strolled down the hallway, away from the waiting room and nursery, lighting a cigarette to pass the time. The end of the corridor was not well lit, and as he approached an apparent right-angle turn he could hear from around the corner two voices in argument.

"Now, I've told you," the male voice said wearily, "there was nothing more we could do. We did our best. I'm sorry."

A woman's voice replied, an older woman, speaking in Chinese. *Cantonese, very likely*, Henry thought, *but I can't make out any of the words.*

A second female voice joined the conversation, speaking English in soothing tones.

"We understand that you're upset, but the doctor has other patients to attend to." This was followed by a muffled reply and a sob, then the sound of footsteps slowly receding down the right-hand hallway.

Unable to see the actors in the small drama and unwilling to intrude on them, Henry stood mystified, smoking and wondering what physical or mental affliction was causing this woman such distress.

Suddenly, around the corner came Dr. K., head down as though in deep thought. Henry stepped aside to avoid him, and the doctor looked up and paused.

"Ah, Mr. . . . . that is, the brother of the new mother, I presume?"

"Chan, Henry Chan, that's right." He gestured toward the hallway from which the doctor had come. "I was just having a cigarette here, and—"

" —and no doubt you heard something of the little difficulty a few minutes ago?" Dr. Klindleman looked keenly at him.

"Well, yes, I did as a matter of fact," Henry stammered. "It sounded rather distressing. For the woman, I mean."

Dr. K.'s professional demeanor transformed his face as though a switch had been thrown.

"A sad case, but a very interesting one. One of your distant kinsfolk, so to speak, speaks only Chinese, so we have struggled to communicate with her." He sighed. "As best we can determine, she was the mother of a patient—a charity case who died in childbirth. Most unfortunate."

"She sounded quite upset," Henry replied.

"You speak Chinese?" Dr. Klindleman said eagerly. "Perhaps you understood more of what she was saying than we did—that might be of some help."

"I'm afraid I don't," Henry said sheepishly. "My Chinese language skills are not what they should be."

Dr. K. reached under his delivery room gown and withdrew a cigarette, accepting a light from Henry before replying.

"Thank you," he said gratefully, exhaling a cloud toward the hallway ceiling. "It's been a long day."

"The woman," Henry repeated, "was she trying to—"

"She was trying to take charge of her daughter's body," the doctor cut in, his face flushed. "And I had to explain—try to explain—that since we had no record of any next of kin, her daughter's body and the body of the stillborn child turned over to the county for burial, in accordance with hospital policy."

Henry was shocked and at a loss for words.

"The language barrier only added to the difficulty of the conversation," Dr. Klindleman went on, his voice trembling. "In the case of indigent patients we're not given a choice, and apparently we were unaware of this woman's existence."

He cleared his throat and ground the remains of the half-smoked cigarette under his heel. Henry tried to change the subject, but no appropriate topic was forthcoming.

"Very sad," he offered at last. "And difficult for you, I'm sure—both professionally and personally."

The doctor sighed and then turned a brighter expression toward Henry.

"Thankfully, happy outcomes are more common in my profession," he said with a smile, "and I can congratulate you as a new uncle—first time, I assume?"

"Yes, thank you—first time," Henry was still rattled by the grim nature of the doctor's confidences. *And why did he unburden himself to me*, he wondered.

"By the way, thank you for listening to a harried medical man," Dr. K. said awkwardly, as though in answer to Henry's thought. "Sometimes it helps to confide even in a small way to a layman—someone who's not dealing with these matters constantly."

"Not at all," Henry returned. "Your profession must be very . . . rewarding."

"That it is, my boy, that it is." He glanced at his watch. "Well, I must get back to matters at hand. Please excuse me."

Dr. Klindleman departed and Henry followed slowly toward the nursery and waiting room.

Chapter Ten

REDDER IN THE FACE

T he excitement of the day made the calm of the evening
in the Winterslip household all the more inviting. New
father and grandparents eventually had had their fill—for the
time being—of observing the new Winterslip through the
hospital glass, and Henry rejoined them just in time to learn
that mother and child would be patients for several days as was
typical of maternity cases. There was, therefore, nothing for it
but to seek rest and refreshment in a less institutional setting.

"You are welcome to whatever's in our larder, and Rose has
been accumulating provender in anticipation of this present
need, so have at it," John Quincy insisted. Accordingly, having
done justice to a simple meal, host and family guests relaxed
in the comfort of the home's modest furnishings. Soon Mrs.
Chan bade the others goodnight and retired to the guest bedroom, and Henry saw his opportunity.

"Dad, something else has happened that makes me . . . well,
wonder about the hospital," he began. "I'm beginning to think
more seriously about what you always say, how 'Chinese are
psychic people.' "

In as few words as possible, Henry recounted the overheard
hallway incident and Dr. Klindleman's explanation of it. Chan
and John Quincy listened with interest.

"Good heavens—what a hellish situation!" Winterslip exclaimed. "Why on earth did the good doctor tell you all about
it with so little prompting?"

Henry nodded.

"That's what I wondered at first, but then I thought: Maybe he believed that I understood what the woman was saying, and he wanted to explain the whole thing to put the best possible light on it."

Winterslip considered this possibility.

"Maybe. The whole thing seems fishy to me. What do you think, Charlie?"

Chan's face was grave. "Like Henry I am struck by possible psychic feeling," he declared. "Very troubling events, especially for those not used to medical profession that concerns itself with life and death decisions." He paused for a moment. "Suggest you both keep eyes and ears open while visiting Rose and granddaughter tomorrow.

As for me," he consulted a calendar in his pocket notebook, "I have an appointment with old friend in the police department on another matter. But if opportunity presents itself, I will ask his opinion of famed hospital and its Dr. Klindleman."

Henry was relieved. "I feel like we should do something, but I don't know what. But whether I've got a psychic feeling or not, something about 'the good doctor' seems too good to be true to me."

John Quincy replied with a good-natured snort; he sometimes made light of his brother-in-law's detective aspirations. The real detective in the room weighed in, playing family peacekeeper.

"Both points of view may share some truth in this matter," Charlie Chan offered. "To determine which is correct—that is the difficulty." He grinned. "We must seek what the lawyers call, 'preponderance of evidence.'

"Meanwhile," he concluded, rising from the living room davenport, "I must bid you good night. I am weary from travel, and tomorrow promises both business and pleasure."

"Why? What's tomorrow?" Henry inquired.

"Saturday," his father replied, the corners of his mouth turning upward. "And were you not listening? Tomorrow, I take the opportunity to renew acquaintance with venerable police colleague and past collaborator."

It had been several years since Chan's last visit to the decades-old Hall of Justice, a rather grim gray-stone multi-story building that was home to police headquarters, criminal courts, the city prison and the morgue. He looked back with some fondness on his earlier encounters there, especially those with a certain Captain Flannery.

Chan recalled with amusement Flannery's bluster and skepticism during their first investigation together, the murder of Sir Frederic Bruce. Gradually Flannery had come to respect Chan, referring to him as "the best detective west of the Golden Gate."

Now, as the Chief had told him, he would once again work with the redoubtable Flannery or, more likely, one of his underlings. Surely, Chan reasoned, a deputy chief of police would have better things to do than chase down clues with a visiting detective!

The deputy chief's office hummed with activity, uniformed officers coming and going. Charlie presented himself to the official gatekeeper, a secretary whose demeanor echoed the serious nature of police work. *She would keep all these men in line with ease*, Chan thought. *Contrast with more relaxed Honolulu department could not be greater.*

"Inspector Chan, as I live and breathe!" Flannery, emerging from an inner office, looked much the same as Charlie Chan remembered—if anything, more so: a bit stouter, grayer and redder in the face. The deputy chief grasped his visitor's hand and shook it enthusiastically.

"It *is* still Inspector, right? Unless you've been promoted again," Flannery boomed. "Can't keep a good detective down, I always say."

"Heart leaps with joy at sight of old comrade in difficult investigations," Chan replied, wincing slightly from Flannery's grip. "Happily still hold rank of Inspector, thank you," he confirmed, his hand still a prisoner, "but you—you have risen far and now rejoice in grand title and important office. Please accept my heartfelt congratulations."

"Well, thanks, Charlie," Flannery's face grew even a shade redder. "Come in, come into the office! No sense us standing out here jawing like two old-timers."

After ordering coffee for two from a subordinate, then barking a jesting remark at a passing officer, Flannery led the way into a large office that reflected his bluff, vigorous personality. Chan looked around approvingly at the solid wood desk and chairs, a plain rug on the floor, framed citations on the wall behind the desk, and a ceremonial uniform and cap hanging from a corner coat-tree, along with a holstered service revolver.

Flannery gestured toward a chair and leaned on the edge of his desk, his favorite resting stance. The grim-faced secretary delivered coffee in two cups to a small table positioned between the two policemen.

"Just like old times, eh, Charlie?" Flannery sipped the steaming liquid. "I want

to thank you for taking time out from your visit this way. I had a wire from your Chief, confirming that you could maybe help us out with this—this—"

Chan stifled a grin as he recalled Flannery's passion and frustration from past occasions. "Happy to help brother policemen during family visit."

"Family!" Flannery struck the arm of his chair with the flat of his hand. "Say, your Chief's telegram said something about a grandchild! What about it, Charlie?"

Chan beamed. "Pleased to report mother and daughter are well in Lane Hospital maternity ward at present after small offspring's arrival late yesterday afternoon."

"Well, that's grand, Charlie. I would've offered you something stronger than coffee to mark the occasion if I'd been thinking straight." His expression sobered. "Truth is, I'm up against it—hard to keep your mind in order when things are stirred up the way they've been here lately. Your Chief shared my letter, I'm guessing, so you know the lay of the land?"

Chan finished his coffee and placed the cup in its saucer. "Always helpful to hear facts of a case from one most expertly acquainted with same," he replied.

Flannery crossed his legs and exhaled noisily.

"You probably know enough of San Francisco history—and Chinatown's—so I won't give you a lecture," he began. "It's enough to know that what's happening now is just the latest installment in a story that goes back nearly a hundred years. First opium. Then morphine, the 'miracle drug.' " Flannery snorted. "Some miracle! Now, heroin."

The deputy chief stretched out his arm and retrieved a manila folder from his desk.

"Heroin is nothing new here, but now we're seeing more of it. A lot more."

He pulled a sheaf of papers from the folder, handing them to Chan. "Here's a copy of the latest information our boys pulled together. You can read the details for yourself—a lot of facts and figures, as many as we can determine, or estimate—but the bottom line is that we need someone with your background, your experience, to look into certain aspects of the trade. Where's it coming from? Mostly Honolulu, we think. How's it getting through customs or around the inspection process? Where's it being distributed once it gets here? And where does the money go?"

Chan had listened intently, his eyes narrowing at the words, "your background, your experience," but he waited patiently for his host to pause.

"Small-time traffickers, customers in opium dens—we've been dealing with them for as long as I've been with the department, and longer than that, of course," Flannery went on, "but the situation now—hell, these people, whoever they are, they're bad, Charlie. Careless of human life. Flooding the Bay area with the stuff, and beyond that it looks like we've become a port of entry for heroin that finds its way all across the country.

"The department's not taking this lying down, and neither am I," he growled. "These people, whoever they are—I mean to get 'em, and I need your help to do it. What do you say?"

Charlie Chan raised his gaze from the material Flannery had given him. A far-off look was in his eyes, but the moment passed. His black eyes snapped to attention, focusing on the deputy chief.

"Please forgive blunt talk, but to hear 'Chinatown' and then glowing report of my 'background and experience,' those words rang unpleasantly in my ears. For one of my origin they might suggest that you wish to send a 'Chinaman' to spy on his countrymen," he concluded. "Please tell me that this is not so."

Flannery's usually florid countenance had reddened even further, and he hastened to reassure the detective.

"Not only is it not so, Charlie, it didn't even cross my mind that you would take it that way," he cried. "Great Scott—why, I blame myself for not thinking of that, first thing.

"No," he insisted, "the truth of the matter is we need someone who's familiar with the main mode of travel between here and your islands, and that someone has to be experienced enough in police work to poke around any and all parts of the city—wherever the investigation takes us.

"Believe me," Flannery said in a voice that lacked his usual bluster, "I'm just an old beat cop who's climbed through the ranks, and I know that this case needs someone who's not only a good cop and a great detective, but someone who's got that extra something, that intuition—"

"Psychic ability, maybe?" Chan said with a smile.

The tension was broken. Flannery laughed.

"Well, as I seem to recall, you've mentioned something about Chinese people being psychic more than once before," he affirmed. "Me, I was thinking more about your down-to-earth abilities—but if you want to use a crystal ball, that's fine by me, too."

The telephone on Flannery's desk jangled. He stood and picked up the receiver, answering tersely and hanging up almost immediately.

"I'm sorry, they're waiting for me—some blasted meeting and all the brass are there, so—"

"You, too, are 'brass' now, sharing the burdens of leadership," Chan cut in, "but you are skilled, determined, you have understanding, so, as old Chinese saying puts it: What possible difficulty would you have in governing?"

"Meaning I'm the right man for the job?" Flannery laughed. "I guess we both are, Charlie—we're both well suited to the work that's facing us."

He tossed the folder on his desk and took the uniform jacket from the coat-tree.

"As I said, the nuts and bolts of what we know—and what we suspect—are in that report I gave you." He fastened the dark-blue jacket's row of brass buttons as he spoke. "There's one thing that's not there, not written down anywhere since we just learned it last night."

Chan rose from his seat as Flannery took his eight-point chief's hat from the rack and donned it.

"It's a small thing—something one of our informants said, and we don't know what it means. If it means anything," he added. "This fellow was in the drunk tank, then the infirmary where he went down and down. Fortunately I had a man by his bedside just before he—well anyway, the officer was trying to get to the how and why of our case.

Chan waited patiently. Flannery frowned.

"This particular informant, he had never led us astray before, but he was also fond of his joke—especially when in his cups, as he was then," he went on. "Like me he was an old Irishman, and as near as the officer could make out, he mumbled something that sounded like 'old bootlegger new shebeen' and then laughed till he nearly choked."

Seeing Chan's uncomprehending look Flannery hastened to explain.

"You probably have a different name for them in Honolulu," the deputy chief said. "For Irish folk here and back in the old country, a shebeen is an unlicensed establishment—any place that's selling hooch and cheating the tax man."

"Word is new to my English vocabulary," Chan admitted. "Bootleggers are well known to me—were well known," he corrected. "Reference to bootlegger seems strange since social experiment of Prohibition ended some years ago.

"Stranger still," the detective continued, "was laughter of dying man—meaning is clear to you, perhaps?"

Flannery shook his head. Frowning under the brim of the uniform cap he looked even more formidable than usual.

"Our man insists he was talking about the heroin business, but how he knows that I'm sure I don't know . . . Maybe the fella was drunk and delirious."

He shrugged.

"As I said, maybe it means something, maybe not. I know it's not much, Charlie, but by heaven—I've seen you do more with less."

Chan bowed.

"Small things present one at a time, like bits of sand," he began.

"Is that so?"

"In country called Tibet, neighbor to China, monks practice ancient art to create sand paintings called *mandala*, adding many colored bits of sand to create pattern.

"Like small clue you have given me," he continued. "Each bit of sand by itself is nothing. But when all are arranged properly, big picture tells complete story."

Flannery scratched the back of his head and frowned. Asian art and complicated metaphors were a bit off the subject for him.

"Well, Charlie—it's your case, and I'm behind you all the way. Beyond that—"

Chan grinned.

"You are most patient, listening to long-winded man from small island. I must ask for further patience while investigation takes shape, and together we decide which bits of sand to arrange—and which to ignore. Words of drunken man about illegal activity, perhaps, may be taken at face value.

"The snake that sheds its skin is still a serpent."

Chapter Eleven

A SPLASH AND A CRY

Detective Sergeant John Patrick Bigley was eager and willing. He had walked a beat long enough before his recent promotion to be grateful for the opportunity to use his brains as well as his feet.

The call from the deputy chief had surprised him, and his new assignment thrilled him. Who had not read about the Chinese detective from the Hawaiian islands? To be selected, singled out, to be even a small part of an investigation in which such a well-known figure was involved—why, it was the greatest thing that had happened to him in his career!

Short in stature (but tall enough to meet the department's height requirement, he always pointed out to anyone who asked), Bigley was fresh-faced, sandy-haired and clean shaven, with a broad face and narrow jaw. His eyes sparkled with an enthusiasm equaled by a keen wit that he was apt to employ even in the most serious situations—much to the chagrin of his superiors.

Bigley sat outside the deputy chief's office waiting for the meeting inside to end.

The door opened suddenly, and he jumped to his feet.

"Ah, there you are, Bigley," Flannery cried. "Charlie, since I won't be able to spend as much time on this matter as I'd like, I've arranged for this up-and-coming officer to assist you.

"Detective Sergeant Bigley, meet Inspector Chan of Honolulu. I know the two of you are going to hit it off in a big way."

The two shook hands as Bigley exclaimed, "This is a real honor for me, Inspector. I'm just as pleased as I can be to work alongside you and hopefully be of some help."

Chan bowed.

"I am overwhelmed at hospitality of the department and grateful for opportunity to experience latest techniques of policing from one whose career only ascends from this point on."

"That's very kind of you, Inspector Chan," Bigley smiled broadly. "I've been called a rookie before, but never in such swell language."

The three men laughed.

"Don't you listen to him, Charlie," Flannery declared. "Bigley's sharp, and he knows the city. He's just the man for your job. As for you, Bigley," he said sharply, "I expect big things from you—so don't disappoint me. Is that understood?"

The young detective saluted. "Yes, sir—I won't let you down."

The deputy chief cracked a smile and slapped Bigley on the shoulder.

"Good man! Well, Charlie—thanks again for taking this on. I've got to be getting along now, but I'll be seeing you."

Flannery departed, and a brief but awkward silence descended.

"Well—er—where would you like to begin, Inspector?" Bigley said nervously. "The deputy chief told me this is about the dope racket, but is there anywhere in the city you want to go, people you need to see? I have a car waiting."

Before Chan could reply, a uniformed officer approached.

"Inspector Chan? There's a call for you—you can take it at this station." He pointed to a black candlestick telephone on a nearby vacant desk.

Chan nodded and grasped the phone, pressing the receiver to his ear.

"Inspector Chan? Hold please," a tinny female voice commanded. A series of clicks ensued.

"Dad? It's Henry. Glad I caught you there."

"Have just concluded meeting," Chan said loudly, attempting to compete with noise on the other end of the line. "I am leaving Hall of Justice shortly with new partner. Henry—difficult to hear you clearly, where are you?"

"I got a note from the crewman I told you about, Notley, and I think something has happened to him." An industrial clattering drowned out Henry's voice for a few seconds, as Chan strained to hear.

"—something must've happened because it seemed to me from the note and what he said earlier that he was trying to reach you through me. The note says he had information that would interest you."

"Henry, connection is very bad—I will come to you, tell me where you are."

"I'm at the pier where the *Monterey* is laid up, Pier 32. See you soon—and thanks, Dad."

The detective cradled the phone and turned to Bigley.

"Please excuse this brief interruption, but that was my eldest son, Henry, who was approached by an officer on the *Monterey* wishing to discuss confidential matter," Chan explained. "This may be side path on the way to our investigation—but sometimes detective must be like switchboard operator," he gestured at the desk telephone, "available to all, ready to respond to any call—to make use of all situations that may provide useful information.

"Since our task is to determine means of shipping certain items across Pacific waters, Pier 32 may be good place to start."

"At your service, Mr.—I mean, Inspector—what should I call you?"

"Since we are now collaborating as fellow detectives, suggest that we adopt American custom and use first names," Chan replied as the two made their way out of the building. "Deputy Chief Flannery did not share your full name with me, so—"

"It's John Patrick Bigley, Inspector—er, Charlie—but 'John Patrick' is quite a mouthful, so the boys in the department call me 'J.P.'"

"Excellent initials for one devoted to law and order," Chan noted with a grin, as they climbed into a black sedan in front of the Hall of Justice, "since it can also stand for 'Justice of the Peace.'"

Henry Chan was waiting near the pier shed where he had claimed the family luggage a few days ago when his father and Detective Sergeant Bigley arrived. Introductions completed, the two Chans compared notes.

" . . . so," the detective told his son, "Deputy Chief Flannery has asked for help to probe smuggling activities taking place, it is thought, between Honolulu and San Francisco. Detective Sergeant Bigley—J.P.—is on assignment so that aged detective does not lose himself in this vast city.

"Tell me more about this Notley and his message to you."

Henry pulled the note from his coat pocket and handed it over.

"The man who brought it said he was a seaman aboard the *Monterey*," Henry explained. "He took it to Calico Jim's, and Jimmy Moran—that's the owner—called me. I left my number with him in case Notley showed up there.

"Well," the younger Chan went on, "the fellow who gave Moran the note said Notley insisted he wait forty-eight hours before delivering it. If he didn't turn up before then, they were to assume something had happened."

Chan frowned.

"Note says this Notley feared discovery by those he would betray in smuggling business. But he names no names, promising to speak in full when meeting occurs."

The detective handed the paper to Bigley, who read it over eagerly.

Their conversation was interrupted by a flurry of activity at a nearby pier shed. Several customs inspectors were among the knot of men gathered at the entrance, next to a stack of luggage.

"Bigley!"

One of the uniformed customs officers advanced, extending his hand.

"Well, now—Officer McRory, is it? Fancy seeing the likes of you here," Bigley cried. "I'd heard you left the department to move on up to bigger and better things."

"Now, then, look at your own self—Detective Sergeant John Patrick Bigley! What a wonder it is, to be sure," the officer returned admiringly, gazing at J.P.'s fedora.

"What, exactly, is so wondrous about my hat?" Bigley said suspiciously.

"Why, that it will so easily accommodate your swollen head, J.P. Plainclothes!" McRory burst out laughing, and the red-faced Bigley grinned good-naturedly, thumping his old comrade on the chest with a fist. "No one would have predicted that two flatties poundin' a beat five years ago would end up where we are," J.P. grinned, "and that's for sure."

"You sure got on this case quick enough," marveled the customs officer, gesturing at the activity behind him. "But the big boys will tussle over this one. Is it a local matter, something for our federal friends—or both?"

"Case?" Bigley was mystified. "You got me wrong this time. Here, let me introduce you to the reason for my visit to this lovely district."

Taking McRory by the arm, he turned to Chan and performed the necessary office.

"Not the Inspector Chan who's been in the papers hereabouts for years?" McRory shook the detective's hand with the enthusiasm of a chamber of commerce booster. "This is a real pleasure, Mr. Chan."

"The honor is mine," Chan replied graciously, bowing slightly. "Pleased to observe happy reunion of friends.

"Allow me to make known to you Henry Chan, my eldest son. Like me, he is here in unofficial capacity."

"Say, what's this case that you think I already know about?" Bigley interjected in the middle of the handshaking. "Since we're here, you might as well clue us in."

"Come along into the shed," McRory replied, walking toward a row of tables with luggage lined up in various stages of unpacking. Two other customs agents nodded as McRory made brief introductions. "Here's the item that attracted our interest."

He pointed to a seaman's kit bag, its contents by its side.

Amid the worn clothes and ordinary personal items was a tiny tin box, lid ajar, brimming with a white powder.

Chan examined the contents carefully, dabbing the tip of his right forefinger into the powder and tasting a miniscule sample.

"Famous Chinese surgeon Hua To used distant ancestor of this preparation on patients before operating on them," he remarked. "Ancient Greeks also thought opium from poppy plants had medical value. Later, Chinese mixed it with tobacco and smoked same."

"Opium's something that the old-timers talk about mostly as part of the city's history—the bad old days, before the big fire burned a lot of it out," Bigley offered. McRory nodded. Opium was old news.

"Fiery event destroyed much and killed many," Chan responded. "Opium, gambling, violent men—Chinatown had acquired an evil name, along with Barbary Coast. But great fire alone did not prevent science from finding new ways to turn poppy plant into deadly burden for generations to come.

"Skillful German scientist discovered most powerful part of opium and named it after Greek god Morpheus, god of dreams," said Chan. "God of nightmares would be more appropriate divinity responsible for misery associated with present-day use of morphine and its terrible offspring."

Henry was mystified. He had spent his young life far from the decadence of the nightclub and weekend party life in America and Europe, where some of his well-to-do contemporaries had trifled with drugs over the last decade.

"I don't get it, dad. What's this stuff for, if not medicine?"

McRory and Bigley grinned; Charlie Chan sighed. American slang plagued his offspring despite his attempts to instill in them respect for proper English.

"So many words of English language available to you, and still you employ crude expressions such as 'get it' and 'stuff,'" he chided, shaking his head.

Henry shrugged. His father's disdain for slang was nothing new.

"This 'stuff' worth far more to criminals who sell it to growing number of addicted persons," Chan said grimly. "What doctors use to treat suffering patients becomes deadly burden for customers of lawless salesmen."

Charlie Chan held up the tin box by way of illustration.

"Morphine powder easy to smuggle when shipped with other powders, and when it arrives at destination powder can be sold—or turned into more valuable, more dangerous drug.

"Heroin."

"You mean, this stuff—sorry!—this *powder* is coming off ships here in San Francisco so that it can be turned into heroin? But who's buying it? Where does it all end up?"

Bigley stirred.

"If we could answer all those questions, this job would be easy," he remarked. "The department wants to see if we can turn off the spigot—figure out how the goods are gettin' here and stop the flow. That's where we think Inspector Chan can help shed some light."

Charlie Chan returned the tin box to its resting place in the seaman's kit bag.

"Well-organized effort to bring to this country opium product in powdered form must be the work of many," he replied. "Final destinations could be anywhere in cities where demand for harmful drugs presents opportunities for illegal profits.

"Middleman could be highest bidder in criminal marketplace," said Chan, "but answers to all questions such as these still to be discovered. This small metal container is only one link in middle of long chain."

McRory consulted a pocket-sized notebook.

"This bag was found aboard the *Monterey* in a locker belonging to the assistant steward," he noted. "A Mr. Notley."

Charlie Chan and Henry exchanged knowing looks.

"I was just going aboard to speak to this Notley," McRory said. "Care to come along, gentlemen?"

The four men headed toward the *Monterey*'s gangplank as a seagoing Santa Claus descended it. Ship steward "Wild Bill" Craxton's grim expression did not bode well for anyone who encountered his wrath, but he was familiar with McRory and greeted him with official courtesy.

"Mr. Craxton, a pleasure to see you again," McRory began. "These gentlemen and I would like to have a word with a member of the crew, the fellow Notley—he's under your authority, I understand?"

Wild Bill had opened his mouth to reply when a splash and a cry of "Man overboard!" split the air. "Ahoy on the pier! Throw him a line, he's going under!"

The men hurried toward the edge of the pier in the direction of the splash.

"I see him," cried Henry. "He's in trouble!"

The younger Chan flung off his jacket, kicked off his shoes, and dove into the water as the other men shouted words of caution and encouragement. The noise soon attracted a crowd, and all eyes were on the water.

Seconds ticked by. McRory located a rope and preserver, which he prepared to cast into the water. The onlookers murmured anxiously. Only Charlie Chan remained calm—outwardly, at least.

"There they are!"

A voice in the crowd broke the uneasy silence, and McRory hurled the life preserver toward the two heads that had emerged from the dark water. Henry's flushed and strained face was visible, but the other man was apparently unconscious. The younger Chan towed his inert charge toward outstretched hands, and the two were soon pulled onto the pier.

Charlie Chan was at his son's side in an instant. Satisfying himself that Henry was unharmed he turned his attention to the other man, who lay unmoving as Craxton attempted to revive him. The chief steward's ministrations were as gentle as his general demeanor.

"Come on, blast your hide—take a breath," he thundered, pressing down on the man's abdomen. Craxton had the first-aid training common to able-bodied seamen, even if his bedside manner was a trifle unorthodox. "You'll not escape duty through such a stunt as this, damn your eyes."

A gurgling expectoration of water from the man's mouth answered Craxton, prompting a collective sigh of relief from the crowd.

"He ain't dead, not by a long shot," declared Craxton, rising to his feet. "He just needs more doctorin' than I'm capable of."

A somewhat-out-of-breath Bigley pushed through the crowd, "I've called for an ambulance," he put in, gasping. "Nearest telephone was two blocks away."

Indeed, the clanging of bells heralded the arrival of two medical attendants in a city ambulance, and the man was quickly placed on a stretcher and loaded aboard the vehicle. Charlie Chan turned to Craxton.

"Distressed man a fellow crew member?" he inquired.

"That's just the thing of it," Craxton replied. "You were sayin' you wanted a word with Notley? Well, if he pulls through, I reckon you'll have to talk to him in hospital."

"That's what I wanted to tell you, Dad," Henry cut in, wrapping his dry jacket around his soaked frame. "As soon as I hit the water and could see his head and face, I knew it was Notley.

"And another thing," he went on, lowering his voice. "He looked awful banged up. His face especially—I think somebody gave him a good going-over."

Charlie Chan's expression grew thoughtful.

"Old proverb from Chu says gazing deeply into a pool is unlucky," he intoned, "and the wisdom that reveals secrets can be fatal."

Chapter Twelve

NOTLEY'S QUARTERS

T he crowd slowly dispersed, and the ambulance departed with siren blaring, bound for the same hospital—the Chans realized—where Rose and her newborn were patients.

Detective Bigley took his leave after assuring Charlie that he would be at Notley's bedside should the injured man awaken. McRory, deprived of a suspect to question about the contraband discovered, looked at the Chans. Henry turned to his father, and Charlie Chan cast his eyes again upon the nearby *Monterey*.

"Perhaps now we can resume visit to crewmembers aboard ship that may provide answers to questions about this Notley," he told the other two. "Especially elusive chief steward, who did not linger to determine welfare of his assistant."

Again the Chans and McRory boarded the *Monterey*, this time in search of Wild Bill Craxton. A loafing crewman directed them below deck to a banging, clattering engine room where workers were generating nearly equal amounts of noise, smoke and sparks.

Their quarry was easy to spot—and to hear. Craxton's pipe was adding fumes to the hellish atmosphere as he loudly exchanged words with a greasy-faced individual who appeared to be the ship's engineer. Seeing the delegation of three approaching, Wild Bill growled something at the engineer and walked toward Charlie Chan.

"Well?" The single word barked at the Chans and McRory was more challenge than question. Craxton's beard bristled as he puffed his pipe; he was master here, they were mere interlopers.

"Regret the necessity of interrupting your many duties on board magnificent vessel," Chan began calmly, raising his voice to compete with the racket. "No doubt you have made the acquaintance of Officer McRory of the customs agency." Craxton acknowledged the customs man with a curt nod. "Permit me to introduce myself: I am Charlie Chan, detective inspector of Honolulu police, and this is my son Henry."

Craxton pulled the stem of the pipe out of his mouth long enough to acknowledge the introductions with a grunt, and a terse, "Bill Craxton, chief steward on the *Monterey*. What can I do for you gents?"

Chan bowed slightly.

"Unfortunate injuries to your assistant prevent us from speaking directly to him about matters of great concern to shipping authorities, so we have come to ask that you conduct us to his quarters so that we may examine same."

Wild Bill's brow creased, his normally surly expression changing to an indifferent scowl.

"Why not? You'll find precious little there that our friends in customs haven't already had their way with," he said through the pipe smoke. "As many years as I can count I've been on this run, and this is the first time the crew has been treated like a lot of crooks."

McRory cleared his throat.

"Special measures put in place recently—orders from above—and we've been conducting more thorough inspections of crew baggage, in addition to passenger belongings and any cargo," the customs man explained. "Certain bags were taken off when the *Monterey* first docked, and that's how we came to be looking at Notley's kit."

"Little enough cargo you'd be findin' on a passenger ship like the *Monterey*," Craxton pointed out. "All you've done, as far as I can see, is rifle bag and baggage of honest seamen, including that blasted Notley."

"And whatever *he's* been up to," Craxton added with an oath, "is nothing to do with his official duties, the ship or the company."

Favoring all three men with a kind of summary frown seasoned with smoke, Wild Bill turned and exited the engine room with a wave of his arm indicating that they should follow.

Notley's quarters consisted of a bunk and a kind of nook shaped by the bulkhead. Personal touches were absent. The customs man turned over the tiny bunk's bedding, and a folded rectangle of old paper fell between his feet.

"Well, now, what's this?" McRory exclaimed, picking up and unfolding a tattered and yellowing handbill. The Chans looked on as he glanced at it; first one side, then the other.

It was evidently a promotional effort for some long-ago theatrical production. Bold type proclaimed a limited run for a three-act farce called "Charley's Aunt," and a photograph of the play's costumed cast—three men, three women—vied for attention with glowing quotes from enthusiastic critics.

"This Craxton must've fancied the theater, I guess," McRory said, looking toward Will Bill Craxton for affirmation. Showing no interest in their find, Wild Bill was recharging his pipe and preparing to thicken the already close atmosphere. .

"Kept himself to himself, he did," Craxton grunted.. "I never saw him ashore, but he mentioned a tavern more than once—Calico Jim's—that's more likely where he spent his time."

McRory handed the faded poster to Charlie Chan and turned his attention back to the bunk and the rest of Notley's tiny quarters. Chan scanned the handbill and turned it over. On the back were three short rows of figures written in pencil, followed by a faint underline and crude drawings of two squares of different sizes.

"Three, seven, nine, five," Henry read from the first line. "And those same four numbers repeated twice."

Charlie Chan's face remained impassive as he scanned the numbers.

"Note line under three identical numbers—three-thousand, seven-hundred and ninety-five. Could have been start of addition problem left unfinished," the detective noted. "Author may have intended to tally three equal shares of—dollars?."

"Well, whatever it is, it don't seem to bear on the current situation," the customs man remarked dismissively. "I've seen all I need to see."

Chan nodded, folding up the old paper and pocketing it for further examination later.

"If there's nothing else, " Craxton growled, "I've got a job to do. Seems to me you'd best be talkin' to the man himself if you want to know what he's been up to."

Chan turned toward the impatient steward and nodded.

"Excellent suggestion, one that we will pursue when injured man awakens in hospital bed."

Craxton blew out his cheeks and turned to lead his guests out of his assistant's quarters.

"One question, please," Chan put in. "You and this Notley make many voyages together?"

"More than a few on this run over these last five years or more, I reckon," Craxton replied grudgingly. "Why d'you ask?"

Chan's bland expression complemented his calm response.

"Often those working together in close quarters for years learn much of their companions," he replied. "Curious that you know so little of assistant whose work surely required collaboration, perhaps frequent conversation."

The already gruff countenance of the ersatz Santa Claus darkened further. There would be coal in Charlie Chan's stocking if this Saint Nick were on duty.

"I told you," he thundered, "Notley kept to himself on shore. On board ship, he minded his business—and I had no time for making friends with him or any other member of the crew."

With that, Craxton led the two Chans and McRory to the deck and gangplank, and the three found themselves on shore in short order.

"Well, Inspector? What do you think?" The customs inspector's professional curiosity was evident. He wanted to know if Chan had seen or heard something that had escaped him. "That Craxton's a hard case—no great love for the authorities, that's for sure."

Chan shrugged.

"Irritable man further aggravated by delays that keep ship docked here," he pointed out. "Perhaps he directs his frustration at nearest target, inquisitive men who interrupt his work.

"But," the detective said thoughtfully, "it is curious that quarters of assistant steward Notley show no signs of illicit activity such as those found in his kit bag. And Craxton seems eager to distance himself from assistant."

Henry, who had remained silent in recognition of his unofficial status, broke the brief silence that followed his father's reply.

"Maybe Craxton helped Notley go for a swim? He sure didn't seem at all upset that a man he's worked with for years was badly injured."

McRory scoffed, but Chan took the suggestion seriously.

"True that Craxton expresses no particular fond feeling for fellow crew member," he declared. "What this means, we have yet to discover.

"As for the injured man's journey from deck to harbor waters, perhaps you will recall that Craxton was in view when noise of Notley's arrival in water was heard by us."

"So, Craxton couldn't have given him a shove," Henry acknowledged ruefully. "But surely he didn't just jump in?"

Charlie Chan grinned.

"Sailing man, one who is likely an excellent swimmer would surely not choose drowning to make away with himself," he agreed. "Perhaps even now he is providing explanation of harbor bath to Detective Bigley, who waits at hospital for us to join him."

Henry nodded with some enthusiasm. He had become increasingly interested in observing his father's work on this case, even though he hadn't grasped all its essentials. The younger Chan was looking forward to hearing what the injured Notley had to say.

Taking leave of McRory, who reluctantly returned to pier-shed screening duty, the two Chans motored to the hospital and soon were at the main entrance, where the detective paused for a moment.

"Suggest you rejoin mother and rest of family so that they know we have not forgotten them," Chan said to his son. "Tell Mama that I will see her soon—as soon as possible."

Henry's face fell.

"I was hoping to come with you—to hear what Notley has to say," he protested, but his father interrupted.

"Grateful for your contributions to investigation so far, and it is possible that you will be called on again as developments warrant," said Chan. "Please recall that your first responsibility on mainland is to your mother. All else will come to pass in due course."

Doing his best to conceal his disappointment Henry managed a respectful reply before heading across the lobby to the elevator. Charlie Chan made his way to the information desk to inquire about the injured seaman and his detective watchdog—and to telephone an old San Francisco acquaintance.

Henry Chan was something of an enigma to his mother—perhaps less so to his father. Oldest of eleven children, he seemed more like his parents in some ways than did his younger siblings. He spoke both the old and new languages, Cantonese and English, more fluently than his brothers and sisters, which pleased his mother particularly. In dress and manners he was every bit the young American professional man who worked in an office and aspired to advancement in business, qualities that found favor with both parents.

As gregarious with his friends as he was shy and introspective with family, he quietly honored the older generation and eschewed the bright outspokenness of his sister Rose, whose outward personality appeared far more "American" than his. In reality he was every bit as philosophical as the famous father he admired greatly.

Henry thought that he might one day pursue some line of investigative work, not on the police force, but perhaps as a private detective—following his father's path in a different way. His goal was to strike out on his own and honor the Chan family and his father's famed achievements without joining an organization in which he would always be known as "Charlie's son."

He had not shared his career aspirations with either parent or anyone else, but the current investigation had revived these musings, along with a growing frustration that he was destined to be a mere observer. Still, what role could he play in his father's work? It seemed he was always to be an onlooker, and that would hardly advance his career ambitions.

As he stepped out of the elevator, Charlie Chan heard raised voices and running footsteps. Noting the unattended nurse's station, he walked quickly toward the commotion coming from a room midway down the hall. As he reached the doorway, he narrowly avoided colliding with Detective Bigley emerging from the room with anger and frustration writ large on his face.

"He's gone, Charlie," the detective said glumly. "Never spoke a word."

"Injuries and near-drowning cause death?" Chan said sharply. "Where is doctor?"

"In there with a nurse," Bigley replied. "It's like this, Charlie: He was half-awake in the ambulance on the way here, kept muttering and talking to himself."

"You made note of words spoken by injured man?" Chan inquired.

"It was just gibberish, near as I could make out," Bigley said glumly. "Anyway, when we got here they put him on a gurney and settled him in this room—a nurse gave him a shot to help him sleep—then she left, and I went down the hall to the washroom for a minute or two. When I got back, he wasn't breathing at all. I yelled for a nurse, and a couple of 'em came runnin', but they said he was gone."

Chan nodded and pointed toward the doorway.

"I have great desire to see body, if you would be so kind as to assert official authority," he suggested. "The opportunity to examine victim of possibly suspicious death is rare—not to be neglected."

"Suspicious?" Bigley perked up. "What makes you think so?"

Chan moved toward the room, speaking softly over his shoulder.

"Strange that man involved in criminal activity lands in harbor and dies in hospital just as we are about to question him," he replied. "Events that swarm like bees from disturbed hive not always coincidence."

"Yeah, well I hope we don't get stung," Bigley whispered back.

"Suggest you place call to coroner and request immediate response," Chan murmured calmly .

"Just as soon as we have our look-see," Bigley agreed. Clearing his throat, the detective walked into the room with Chan close behind.

"I'm Detective Bigley from the police department, and this is Inspector Chan," he announced. "We'd like to examine the body of this man."

Chapter Thirteen

"MURDER!"

A young doctor and an even younger nurse looked up from the bedside of the dead man. The doctor frowned.

"That would be rather irregular, but I'm sure you have some reason for intruding in a purely medical matter," he replied. "I'm Dr. Rowland, and this is Nurse Burch. I'll be the attending physician of record as far as the death certificate is concerned."

He paused for an instant; a thought had occurred to him.

"Might we see some identification before you proceed? Purely a matter of form."

Bigley and Chan produced their credentials, and the doctor glanced at them.

"Thank you. Now, if you have no further need of me, I'll—"

"One moment, please," Chan cut in. "You have made preliminary examination?"

"Yes. I'm satisfied that the cause of death was due to acute pulmonary edema—caused primarily by the subject's immersion in water." "You mean he drowned?" Bigley demanded. "But he was breathing on his way here, even said a few words..."

"It's my understanding that this man was submerged for some undetermined amount of time and was not breathing when he was pulled from the water," the doctor replied. "However long he was under water, fluid had ample opportunity to enter the lungs. The intervention, pulling him from the water and reviving him, had only temporary effect. The damage had been done.

"By the time he arrived here, it was simply too late. The water in his lungs resulted in acute edema—noncardiogenic edema, not involving the heart directly. If we had had more time, if he had gotten here sooner," the doctor shrugged, "additional oxygen and an injection might've made the difference. As it was, his lungs failed quite quickly, his heart stopped, and here we are."

Bigley was scribbling furiously in his notebook, trying to translate the medical jargon into plain English, while Chan looked closely at the body, especially the face and head.

"Possible to tell whether these injuries," he said, pointing to several bruises and abrasions on the dead man's face, "occurred before or after he entered the water?"

"I made a note of those," the doctor replied. "It seems likely that at least some of them were inflicted while he was in the water, perhaps from a collision with the side of the boat or ship that I'm told he fell from."

"Or was pushed from," muttered Bigley, signing to Chan that he was going to call the coroner's office.

The doctor glanced at the departing police detective and continued.

"Some of the injuries appear to me a little older than those, maybe suffered before he went into the water. Difficult to say with any degree of certainty."

Chan leaned over the body, moving the head from side to side.

"Did doctor observe this mark on throat?"

Chan pushed aside the skin to reveal a faint thin discoloration, a line that appeared to encircle the neck.

Dr. Rowland reddened as he looked closely at the mark, cursing softly under his breath.

"No—no, I did not. The folds of the neck must've been relaxed enough in pre-rigor to conceal it from view.

"However," the doctor said irritably as he stood up, "it doesn't change the cause of death, and I don't see that it alters my medical conclusions."

"Medically, cause of death remains failure of lungs," Chan replied, "but legally, thin stripe on neck of man police wished to question most urgently points to murder."

"Murder!"

The nurse who had been listening with great interest turned pale and whispered the word as she sank into a visitor chair. The doctor began to protest the detective's conclusion, but Chan ignored the attempt.

"Consider sequence of events," the detective said. "This man travels on ship concerned somehow in criminal activity. He meets son of detective, seeks meeting with him but fails to appear. Customs officials find contraband in his personal effects. Hoping to question him we arrive too late to prevent his unfortunate dive into harbor."

Chan paused. "Finally he arrives here for medical assistance, probably already near death—but mark on throat indicates someone was not willing to leave such matters to chance."

Bigley reentered the room in time to hear most of Chan's summary. The doctor cleared his throat and admitted defeat.

"I was unaware of the background you've described—it all certainly puts things in a different light, and I may have been a bit hasty in my initial examination. However," he added quickly, resuming his earlier tone of irritated self-importance, "Won't this man's death be the subject of an autopsy?"

Bigley took a step forward, as if to remind the gathering that he represented official authority.

"I've put in a call to the coroner, and he's on his way. Based on Mr. Chan's summing up I'm treating this as a suspicious death. So, Doctor—?"

"Rowland."

"So, Dr. Rowland, unless you have anything further to add, I think you're dismissed. Right, Charlie?"

Chan nodded. "Dr. Rowland has been most helpful, providing medical expertise and reminding police of their limited grasp of same." He bowed slightly, and the doctor stalked out of the room.

Chan turned to the nurse.

"Thank you for your patience. To repeat introductions, this gentleman is Detective Sergeant Bigley, and I am Inspector Chan. You are, I think, Nurse Burch?"

"Yes, I'm Edith—Edith Burch."

"You assisted when patient was brought to this room?"

"Yes, the two men from the ambulance wheeled him in, and helped me move him from the gurney to the bed," Nurse Burch replied nervously. "Detective—er—Bigley was with them. The ambulance driver and his assistant left, and I made the patient comfortable."

"The patient was unconscious? Spoke no words?"

"Much of the time he appeared to be unconscious, except....

The recollection of events trailed off as the young woman's pale complexion reddened.

"Except when, please?" Chan persisted. "The importance of any word spoken, any indication from him, cannot be overstated."

"It's just a bit embarrassing," the nurse went on in some confusion. "I was checking the patient's pulse when he grabbed my hand and squeezed. I tried to pull away, but he wouldn't let go. His eyes were open, and he looked me right in the face and—and—he called me . . .

"Baby."

The nurse looked up shyly. In Bigley's estimation she was quite young and had probably just finished her training.

Probably her first job, he thought. *She must've had a sheltered upbringing.*

"It's not that I'm unused to patients saying all manner of things," she explained hastily. "It's just that I've been called that by rude men before, the kind of men who shout and whistle at a girl in public."

Chan nodded sympathetically.

"You think this man awakens and responds crudely to sight of pretty nurse?"

"Yes, it certainly seemed that way to me.""Patient spoke no other words in your hearing?"

"No, after he said that he closed his eyes. And then I was called away."Bigley looked at Chan.

"That's right, Charlie. It's just like she says: He grabs her hand, says 'baby' and goes out like a light. Then since he wasn't talkin' I figured I could step down the hall to the payphone in the waiting area. I called headquarters just to check in and let 'em know the latest.

"When I got back, he looked different—like he'd tried to get out of bed—and he wasn't breathin'. I let out a yell, and folks came runnin', the doctor and Nurse Burch here. And then you showed up just a minute or two later—"

"Excuse my interruption," Chan cut in. "Very important: Did you see anyone in corridor on way to and from telephone?"

Bigley closed his eyes for a moment and wrinkled his forehead in concentration.

"I closed the door behind me, and I headed toward the waiting area . . . almost bumped into a nurse who was standing in the doorway of the next room down the hall. She was talkin' to someone in that room, just passin' the time it seemed like. Then there was two nurses walkin' toward me in a hurry, and then I went through the double-doors and got to the phone. Made my call—""Anyone in waiting area when you arrive at telephone?"

Bigley scratched his head.

"Let me see. There was one old fellow and a couple—man and woman talking to each other—and two . . . no, three other women, younger women. I guess I made a mental note of 'em all as I walked up to the phone. Didn't pay any attention to 'em when I spoke to the desk sergeant. And when I hung up—say!"

Chan smiled.

"Perhaps," he asked Bigley, "fewer persons were waiting than before?"

The police detective's eyes widened.

"Two of 'em were gone!"

Chapter Fourteen

WHAT NURSE MEADOWS RECALLED

C harlie Chan received Bigley's revelation calmly.

"Two persons had departed waiting area near telephone?"

"Yeah! The couple was gone, the rest were still there," Bigley looked at Chan with something like awe. "How did you know?"

"Not through brilliant deduction," Chan assured him. "Many who wait in hospital come and go with great frequency. You are positive that only the man and woman left while you spoke on telephone?"

"Positive," Bigley affirmed, anticipating Chan's next question. "I didn't get a good look at 'em, wasn't thinkin' about people in the waiting area havin' anything to do with Notley. They were just 'middle,' I guess."

"Middle?"

"Middle-aged, middle height and weight," Bigley said sheepishly. "Middle everything. Just average."

Chan nodded.

"Do not assume blame where no fault has occurred," he told the police detective. "Couple who left are worth noting, that is all. Hospital sees constant comings and goings of many people, like disturbed anthill."

Chan turned back to Nurse Burch, whose flushed face had resumed its normal hue.

"You have been most helpful, and we are grateful for cooperation."

"You're welcome," the nurse replied, "Is there anything else I can help you with?"

"Only one more question," said Chan. "You have boss-nurse on this floor, in charge of this area?"

Burch nodded. "Yes, that would be Nurse Meadows. She reports directly to Dr. Klindleman, the head of this department. Meadows is very likely at her station. It's on this floor, in this wing. I can take you there," she offered.

"Thank you so much," Chan nodded. "Only one last question for the moment, please. You said that after injured man spoke one word you were called away?"

"That's right. Nurse Meadows called to me from outside the door that I was wanted in administration," the nurse replied. "But it was rather odd . . ."

Chan looked keenly at the woman.

"Odd in what way, please?"

Edith Burch turned toward the two detectives.

"I reported to the administrative offices, but no one there knew any reason why I should be there. One of the nurses said someone must've been playing a joke on me."

The two detectives exchanged glances.

The nurse led Chan and Bigley down the corridor to the nurse's station and introduced them to Nurse Meadows, who dismissed her subordinate and turned to the two detectives.

"I understand you have some questions about the patient, a Mr. Notley, who died this afternoon? How can I help you?"

Chan glanced at Bigley, who gave him a go-ahead nod.

"Thank you for assisting police in investigation of patient death now considered suspicious—"

"What! Suspicious death?" Meadows was startled. "It was my understanding that the patient was a drowning victim. Was that not the case?"

"Suspicion arises for several reasons, some of which we are not at liberty to share," Chan returned. "Possible murder investigation is in its beginning stages, and cause of death will be determined by coroner."

"That's right, miss," Bigley confirmed. "Inspector Chan and I are just trying to determine who was on this floor, especially in this hallway, who might've had access to the patient's room after he was brought in."

Nurse Meadows' brow wrinkled.

"I was on duty then, but not directly involved with the patient. I was here at my desk most of the time from, well, when I became aware that the ambulance men were transferring a patient to this floor."

She gestured helplessly at her surroundings.

"I guess I can't be of much use since I couldn't see the doorway to that room from the nurse's station," she said apologetically.

"Still, you were in fixed position during vital period," Chan persisted. "Perhaps you can tell us about those who passed by your duty station. Many people come and go during the time in question?"

"It's hard to say. I'm afraid that much of the time my eyes were on paperwork—reports, memos, patient charts—occasionally someone would say hello as they passed by, and I did glance up from time to time, but—"

"Please forgive rude interruption. Maybe you can first recollect voices of those known to you who said words of greeting?" Chan suggested. "Later perhaps you can think only of those you saw when looking up."

"I'll try," the nurse replied. "Let me see. First I heard the elevator bell and the ambulance men talking as they pushed the gurney, and then ..."

"Take time to collect your thoughts," Chan said softly. "Maybe close eyes and picture the scene in your mind. Let remembered sounds speak."

"Yes . . . that helps a bit. The admitting nurse downstairs had called to tell me that the ambulance had arrived with a patient, that he was recovering from injuries sustained while in the water. A 'near-drowning' she called it.

"As I hung up the phone the elevator bell rang, and I heard the two men talking and the sound of them pushing the gurney further down the hall."

The nurse opened her eyes.

"Then I saw Nurse Burch hurrying in that direction. She must've received a call from downstairs as I did."

"Maybe you observed Dr. Rowland going to patient's room?" Chan inquired.

"Yes, but that was much later," Meadows said promptly. "After Nurse Burch went by I tried to focus on my review of patient charts, and I was vaguely aware of some of the girls—the nurses—going past in the opposite direction, away from the room. I think they were on their way to the cafeteria. I remember one saying how hungry she was and another saying she was 'dying for a cigarette,' just casual conversation."

"After these ladies pass by then you observe doctor?" Chan prompted.

"Let me think . . . Oh! I remember now. I was making a note on a patient's chart, and the cleaning woman, Marjorie Crandall, wished me a good evening. She said something like, 'I'm off, see you tomorrow,' as she headed for the elevator. Always leaves on time, Marj does. Then I heard the elevator bell ring—that would have been Marj getting on it. I didn't hear anyone get off, but my eyes were on my work just then."

Her brow furrowed for a moment.

"I suppose it's possible someone could've arrived on the elevator just then and walked quietly down the hall. I just don't recall hearing anything like that."

Nurse Meadows paused and opened her eyes, taking a deep breath and exhaling slowly.

"Beyond that there could have been other people coming and going, and I simply wouldn't have seen or heard them," she acknowledged. "That's all I can recall up to that point."

"Most helpful, thank you," Chan said warmly. "Take a moment and then repeat process for the time remaining in period of keen interest for Detective Bigley and myself."

The nurse closed her eyes once more, and frowned in concentration.

"This is difficult," she began. "I know that hospital staff were back and forth, but I don't recall anyone speaking to me. They must've seen I was concentrating on the never-ending paperwork. I distinctly recall the sounds of one or two people walking past not long after the cleaning matron left—""Toward the room in question or away from it?" Chan put in.

"Both, as I recall, so it must've been two or more people. The next thing I remember is"—her eyes flickered open, focusing on Bigley—"this gentleman's arrival. He asked me what room the injured man was in, and I pointed him in the right direction.

"After that, it's a bit of a blur," she sighed. "I believe someone from the housekeeping staff passed by; I noticed the sound the linen cart wheels make. Also I heard a faint sound far off down the hall toward the waiting area—Walter mopping the floor. You know, the sounds of mopping, the water from the bucket and so on."

She sighed.

"Then a few minutes later the nurses who were on break—I assume it was the same group—came back from the direction of the cafeteria. And then there was a telephone call."

"Call for you?" said Chan.

"No, it was downstairs. They said Nurse Burch was wanted, and could she come to administration right away. I went toward the doorway of the room—"

"One moment, please," Chan interrupted. "Call from downstairs summoning Nurse Burch—you recognized the voice?"

"No, I didn't," Meadows replied. "It was fairly noisy at the time and a bit hard to hear the call."

She paused for a moment.

"It was a gruff kind of voice, and all that was said was, 'Have Nurse Burch report to administration,' something like that—very few words. And then the connection went. A bit rude, I thought at the time, although people's manners are the first thing to go when—"

Nurse Meadows stopped abruptly and her eyes widened.

"Someone wanted to get her out of the room," she cried. "That's what you think, isn't it?"

"Nurse Burch has said no one in administrative offices knew of call requesting her presence there," Chan affirmed. "Easy for someone with knowledge of patient and hospital staff to execute telephone hoax. You could not tell whether call came from inside or outside of hospital?"

"No," the nurse responded promptly. "Sometimes the switchboard operator will speak before connecting an outside call, but often she'll just put it through immediately. I usually try to answer on the first ring."

"Return, please, to what you observed while delivering message to colleague," Chan prompted.

I saw Detective Bigley walking down the hall toward the waiting area—"

"To use the telephone," said Bigley to no one in particular.

"I could see him walking toward the mopped section of the hallway floor and almost called out to him to be careful not to slip," said Nurse Meadows. "But then I saw Walter a few feet ahead bent over his bucket, wringing out his mop, so there was no need for me to warn Mr. Bigley."

"That's right, Charlie," Bigley put in. "The cleaner was there like she says, and the floor further down the hall was still wet in spots."

"Continue, please," Chan said to Nurse Meadows.

"I called to Nurse Burch that she was wanted in administration, then I went back to my station," Meadows concluded.

"Question, please. Did you enter room and observe patient's condition?" Chan looked keenly at the nurse, and Bigley unconsciously leaned forward slightly.

"Why, no, I didn't," the nurse replied. "There was no need, since Nurse Burch was already there. I simply walked close enough to the room to ensure that she would hear my voice, and after she replied I returned to my station.

"Several minutes later I heard a commotion—I think it was Detective Bigley shouting—and shortly after that, Dr. Rowland ran by. I went to see if I was needed, but just as I reached the door of the room Nurse Burch hurried past—I think she had just come off the elevator—so I returned to my post."

Chan nodded.

"This janitor you spoke of—"

"Walter. Walter Jenkins," Meadows supplied. "He's filling in while the cleaning matron is away."

"This Walter Jenkins—could he be summoned here to answer questions?"

"Certainly," said Meadows, picking up the receiver and dialing. "He's usually not far off, probably smoking in the glorified janitor's closet he refers to as his 'office.' "

The nurse waited for several seconds before cradling the receiver with an impatient exclamation.

"No answer! I wonder where he's hiding now—"

Her question was interrupted by the jangle of the phone.

"Hello? Yes, just one moment."

Meadows turned to Chan and handed him the receiver.

"The switchboard is transferring a call for you from police headquarters."

Chan brought the phone to his ear in time to hear a series of clicks followed by a familiar booming voice. "Charlie? This is Flannery—you got that case all wrapped up?" This witticism was followed by Flannery's usual bray of laughter.

Chan laughed politely. He was used to the deputy chief's attempts at humor.

"Sorry to report that my investigation so far is much like towing sinking ship with rowboat—much effort, no progress," he rejoined.

"Is that so? That's too bad. Say, you know I'm only joking. I'm calling to invite you to a little party in my office—a chance to chat with old friends and compare notes about this sinking ship you're trying to tow."

"I would welcome opportunity to share what little I have uncovered so far," Chan replied. "When, please?"

"The sooner, the better," Flannery returned. "If it's not inconvenient. If you'd like, I can send a car for you. How's the newest member of the Chan family?"

"Baby girl Chan and mother are enjoying hospital stay in good health, thank you," said Chan. "Other events at hospital have prevented me from visiting new arrival today—"

"Other events there?" Flannery cut in. "What's going on at that hospital?"

"Better that I deliver the latest information to you in person," Chan said hastily. "Thank you for the offer of automobile, but Detective Bigley continues to serve as capable chauffeur. We will join you shortly."

Chan hung up and addressed Nurse Meadows.

"Detective Bigley and I are summoned to a meeting elsewhere, but I have keen desire to speak with elusive janitor, Walter Jenkins. Before we depart hospital, could we pay a visit to this closet-office of his?"

"Of course," the nurse replied. She led the two men down the hallway and paused at a nondescript door a half-dozen feet from the double-doors Bigley had passed through to get to the waiting area and telephone. Pulling a small ring from a capacious pocket, Nurse Meadows sorted through a half-dozen or more keys, none of which was labeled.

"Just a moment," she said, flushing. "I don't often use this particular key, so—"

Chan grasped the doorknob and turned. The door opened easily with a slight squeak of its hinges. It was dark within, and the detective's first impression was of fetid air within.

Meadows sighed.

"That Walter! He knows our policy is to lock every unattended closet and storage room," she fumed. "When I get hold of him he'll be sorry."

Reaching into the darkness, Chan located a light switch and clicked it on. The illuminated scene confirmed his suspicion.

"Reprimanding janitor now will serve no purpose," he said tersely. "Please—do not enter!"

Peering over the detective's shoulder Meadows and Bigley could see the still body of a man lying in a heap next to a pile of rags, a mop and bucket.

"What's happened?" Meadows whispered. "Is he dead?"

"Oh, he's dead all right," Bigley said brusquely. "Only question is—"

"Answer is 'murder,' " Chan said abruptly. He paused for a second then resumed. "Please excuse rudeness, but look without advancing further into the room."

Bigley craned his neck obediently as Chan gestured toward the body.

"Observe the thin mark on throat visible even from here," Chan replied. "Same method used to silence injured man down the hall."

Meadows withdrew from the closet and leaned against the corridor wall as Chan turned to Bigley.

"Please go to nearest telephone and make two calls, if you would be so kind," he told the police detective. "One, inform

Deputy Chief Flannery that we are delayed but will be with him as soon as events permit."

"Got it," Bigley replied readily. "And the other call?"

Chan turned his gaze from the body in the closet to the detective's youthful face.

"Inform coroner's office of doubly urgent request from hospital—now two bodies await examination."

Chapter Fifteen

THE UNFORTUNATE CUSTODIAN

N ot far from the investigation of two deaths a new mother reveled in the attention paid to her and her newborn babe by happy family members.

Two floors below the double homicide's grim scenes, Rose, Henry, their mother and John Quincy Winterslip had spent a pleasant afternoon in Rose's hospital room, joined periodically by "Baby Girl" Winterslip. ("We're thinking about several names but haven't settled on one yet" was John Quincy's prompt response to anyone who inquired.) Like other new arrivals in the ward, the newest family member spent much of her time in a nearby glass-walled nursery.

As instructed Henry had explained his father's absence, and the new parents took it in stride. Not so the family matriarch. While accustomed to the demands of her husband's work Mrs. Chan on this occasion expressed her dissatisfaction with a short burst of commentary delivered in her native tongue. The brief but energetic Cantonese tirade concluded abruptly when a nurse delivered Baby Girl Winterslip to Grandmother Chan's eager arms.

"I think motherhood agrees with you," John Quincy murmured, taking Rose's hands in his. "You're positively blooming! I predict you'll soon be your old self, only more so. I just wish—"

Winterslip's fond hope went unspoken as he stared at his wife's left wrist. A reddish patch marred its otherwise smooth skin.

"Wish what, dear?" Rose inquired, beaming.

"Oh, nothing," said John Quincy, "I was just thinking that your father is missing out on all the family time we're enjoying.

"I see you've bumped yourself, dear," he said casually, pointing out the little mark. "Or maybe one of the nurse's injections was less than successful—sometimes one can get a little bruise from too much needling."

Rose examined the spot, about the size of a dime, and looked up quickly at her husband.

"It's in the same spot you told me about on Jane Doe's wrist," she whispered. "What does it mean?"

"Now, don't go jumping to conclusions," John Quincy replied gently. "It may be nothing at all. His thoughts raced. *I've got to tell Charlie about this. If Rose was marked the same way as the missing woman then—*

"You're sure?" Rose replied anxiously. "I'll ask the nurse about it, or the doctor, whichever one I see first." She took a deep breath and let it out as a yawn. "Gee—feels like it's time for my nap! Just in time, too, since I believe that visiting hours are about over. We'd best be saying our goodbyes."

"Now, you sleep more," her mother advised, handing the infant to its mother reluctantly. "Need rest to be strong—like your mother."

"That's right, Mama," Rose agreed. "I can think of no better example of a strong mother than you."

The visiting contingent departed for home, and a nurse arrived to return Baby Winterslip to the nursery.

"Oh, nurse—could you please take a look at my wrist?" Rose asked. "I seem to have a—well, I don't know exactly what it is. My husband noticed it."

The nurse examined the mark, and both Rose's arms.

"Any other markings or rash of any kind that you've noticed?"

"No, nothing," Rose replied.

"Well, you may have bumped your wrist or rubbed up against the bed railing in your sleep somehow," the nurse said doubtfully. "I'm sure it's nothing serious. Just mention it to Doctor when you see him next and I'll get some lotion you can put on it to help it heal."

With that, nurse and infant departed, and Rose yawned again. *Funny how just lying in bed all day can be so exhausting*, she mused.

Sleep came swiftly to the new mother.

His peers admired Dr. Robert Klindleman's energy and commitment. Long days at the hospital were common, and it was well known that his idea of relaxation after work was voluntary visitation and consultation at Bay Area clinics, orphanages, soup kitchens—wherever poverty-stricken women and children were to be found.

Dr. K. little cared what his fellow physicians thought of his off-duty pursuits. Oblivious to compliments and criticism he focused on his long-term goals. The doctor was convinced that many of the answers to his research questions, and the means to answer them, lay in the troubled institutions he frequented night after night.

Tonight he returned to a regular stop on his rounds: Homeplace Orphanage, where he was a member of the governing board.

"It's good to see you again," Virginia Lande said warmly, taking the doctor's overcoat and hat and making him welcome in her office. "The children always look forward to your visits as I'm sure you know.

"Please," she gestured toward a worn rocking chair, seating herself behind the office desk. "Can I get you something? Coffee?"

Dr. K. shook his head abstractedly and reached into his breast pocket for a cigarette, which he ignited with the flick of a silver-plated lighter. He looked around the room briefly, drawing deeply on the cigarette as Lande waited patiently. She was used to the doctor's seeming indifference and inability to make small talk. At length his perusal of a room he had seen countless times before ended, and he turned his attention to Lande.

"I hope the children are all well? And your newest arrival, the little fellow—any difficulty?"

"Everyone's quite well, thank you," Lande replied. "The baby's settling in nicely—it's been some time since we had an infant here, but we haven't forgotten how to deal with such a situation, I'm happy to say.

"And we were preparing for two when word came that only one would be coming," she added.

"That's fine, just fine," the doctor replied. "It's good that you can adjust to meet these kinds of temporary needs. Perhaps I should examine the little—boy, isn't it?" Lande nodded. "Then I can pay my respects to the other children," Dr. K. concluded, extinguishing his half-consumed cigarette in a desktop ashtray.

"Splendid!" Lande beamed. "I'll take you to our makeshift nursery, it's on this floor—not far." She rose and led the way through the office door and across a foyer into a small room with a bassinet, changing table and rocking chair.

The sole occupant was not more than a few weeks old, and Dr. Klindleman leaned closely over the tiny sleeping figure as Virginia Lande hovered nearby.

"I'm glad you could take the time to look at the little fellow," Lande said hesitantly. "That is, I've been concerned about his appearance—his sallow skin made me think of jaundice—"The doctor tut-tutted dismissively.

"I think that you're just comparing his skin color to that of your other charges," he reassured the woman. "All the other children here currently are white, I assume?"

"Well, yes," Lande acknowledged. "Of course that's not always the case, but at present ... "

"This young man looks to me to be in perfectly good health," Dr. K. pronounced, transferring the infant to the changing table for the necessary poking and prodding. The abruptly awakened patient demonstrated a healthy pair of lungs, crying lustily in response to the doctor's ministrations. "His skin color," the doctor went on, raising his voice to compete with the wailing, "is completely normal for one of his—er—origin."

"That's a relief," Lande replied. "I thought that was the case, but it's good to have your confirmation. It's so worrying," she fretted, "having an infant with us even for so short a period of time—"

"And you can be assured that what you do, the sacrifices you and the orphanage make for the youngest of your inmates in cases like these, all of it is immensely valuable to my work," the doctor assured her. "Incalculable."

Charlie Chan made a cursory examination of the body, taking care to disturb nothing in the janitorial closet. Nurse Meadows accepted his invitation to look more closely at the discolored face. She identified the victim as the oft-truant janitor, Walter Jenkins, and retreated queasily.

Chan looked closely at the neck and hands of the unfortunate custodian and examined his surroundings, kneeling to dip a finger into a bucket of gray water.

He then retrieved from the floor an errant strand from the mop's head that appeared to have become separated from its fellows, placing it carefully in one of the pocket-sized envelopes he carried to secure potential evidence. Finally he placed the back of his hand against the head of a mop that lay near the legs of the dead man.

Rising to his feet he backed slowly out of the closet looking carefully at the floor as he went.

"Good news, Charlie, I've brought reinforcements."

The voice was that of Detective Bigley, who stood just outside the janitor's closet with another man carrying a black leather bag.

"Turns out," the police detective announced, "that when I went to use the phone at the nurse's station I ran into the good doctor, and he was just finishing up with our first customer. So I invited him to take a walk with me, and here we are."

The coroner—for it was he—stepped forward, extending a hand in greeting.

"I don't know if you recall me, Mr. Chan, but we met a few years ago at the university," he said. "And, as Bigley says, 'here we are'—again."

Chan's face lit up in recognition.

"Happy to renew acquaintance with Dr. Chalmers," he exclaimed. "Only wish that the occasion was social instead of professional."

"You and me both," the coroner returned, smiling. "But the wheels of justice grind on, and I am duty-bound to be an efficient cog therein.

"Now," he said briskly, "before I go into the little room you just came out of, I assume you'd like a quick preliminary on the fellow I just met down the hall?"

"Would be most grateful for expert knowledge and opinion to shed light on mysterious circumstances," Chan affirmed. "All the time acknowledging that information shared is, as you say, 'preliminary,' and subject to change."

"You've said it—that goes for both of these, er, customers of mine," the coroner replied. "You know how it goes, Mr. Chan, the autopsy surgeon's report—that's the official finding, and anything I say at this stage has to be received with a grain of salt."

"Rest assured I will treat your words with appropriate amount of seasoning," Chan assured him.

"That's fine, then," Dr. Chalmers pulled from his black medical bag a small notebook and flipped it open. "Subject number one reportedly spent some time in the water immediately prior to transportation here. Various bruises, abrasions and the like appear to have occurred prior to immersion. Confirmation of cause of death awaits, as I mentioned, the autopsy surgeon taking a look inside, especially at the lungs, but—as you no doubt observed, Mr. Chan—a mark around the throat indicates that someone using a wire or something similar—"

Chan cut in more abruptly than was his custom.

"Maybe even item such as this?"

He opened the evidence envelope and displayed the single orphaned strand he had retrieved from the floor near the body. The coroner peered at it without touching it.

"Possibly, possibly, but personally my first choice would be wire. It's more typical in cases like this, more reliable. Where'd this come from?"

"Not from vicinity of the body you just examined," Chan explained. "I took the liberty of collecting this item just now, near second unfortunate individual."

"Hmm." Dr. Chalmers made an additional note in his little book. "I gather that you think the deaths and the method of bringing them about are connected?"

"I am usually cautious in these matters, like wise men crossing river in winter in ancient Chinese story," Chan conceded, "but in this case am 'playing hunch' as my cousin Willie Chan expresses it."

"I'll take that as a 'yes,' " the coroner said, laughing. "You may well be right, although the weapon, if one can call it that, might just as well have been a twin of the one used down the hall. Or something very like it. As for the item you found, let me take charge of that and we'll see what a laboratory examination tells us."

Chan resealed the little envelope and handed it to the doctor, who assured the detective that he would report any findings as soon as possible.

"Now, where was I?" Chalmers consulted his notes again. "Whatever it was, my best guess is that the perpetrator grasped its ends and applied pressure to the first victim's throat, between the larynx and the subglottic space."

Bigley's hand was up in an instant, and the coroner nodded vigorously.

"I know, I know—let me try it in layman's terms. The larynx—that's the area that contains the voice box, so the victim wouldn't be able to cry out. More important, it's the upper part of the windpipe that connects to the lungs.

"And just below the larynx," Dr. Chalmers soldiered on, in his best medical-lecture manner, "we find the subglottic space. That's right underneath the vocal cords, and it's also the narrowest part of the airway, the upper airway.

"So, if you were going to work mischief in this manner that would be a good place to squeeze or apply pressure with a wire or whatever was used," he concluded.

"Many thanks for preliminary report," Chan said. "Question, please. Would placement of deadly strand require special medical knowledge to achieve desired results?"

The coroner sighed, then smiled.

"There, unfortunately, is where one enters the realm of speculation. Would such knowledge be helpful? Certainly. Could someone be garroted—the French have an elegant-sounding word for everything—I say, could someone be garroted successfully *without* a basic anatomy course? Yes, that is also a distinct possibility."

He paused, tugging at his left earlobe.

"It's also possible that someone grabbed whatever was handy and got lucky—no forethought, no special knowledge."

"Thank you for indulging in brief visit to the speculative realm," Chan responded. "All words from coroner who is also a doctor constitute valuable direction at this stage of investigation."

"I'll second that," Bigley piped up. "Now, doc, how about customer number two?"

"That's my cue," Dr. Chalmers responded briskly. "Show me."

Chapter Sixteen

UNORTHODOX ASSIGNMENT

Assured that the coroner would telephone the detectives with a similar summary report for "customer number two," Chan turned to Detective Bigley.

"Each deadly event quickens pace of events," Chan remarked, "like melting spring snow feeds swift mountain river."

"You said it," Bigley agreed. "You think both deaths are tied to the smuggling case? I know that's the first thing my boss will ask."

"Down, please," Chan instructed the elevator operator. "The answer to your question is, 'yes,'" he told Bigley. "Notley becomes target because he seeks a meeting with son of police detective. Motive for second death not so clear, but location and similar method make connection certain."

"Maybe that janitor saw somethin' he shouldn't have," Bigley mused.

"Very possible," Chan agreed, "but whatever real reason, death of person who cleans hospital hallways is reason enough for us to speak with his boss—as soon as possible."

"That would be the head cleaning matron, an old gal named Marjorie Crandall. Jenkins was filling in for her while she's away visiting her sister in Yountville.

"The nurse on that wing, Meadows, she gave me the sister's number. Thought maybe I could save time and talk to the matron before she gets back from her little trip, but when I called she was running errands for the sister." He consulted his notebook and went on. "I spoke to the sister, a Mrs. Baxter, and left a message."

"Place where sister lives—"

"Yountville."

"This Yountville, it is far from city?"

The two exited the elevator and walked toward the hospital's front doorway.

"Not so far that we couldn't pay the two ladies a little call," Bigley said flatly. "We need to track down anyone and everyone we can—before the next thing happens."

"I would be happy to accompany official representative of police department on housecall," Chan grinned, "as soon as we fulfill important social obligation."

"How's that?"

"You and I have been invited to a party given by Deputy Chief Flannery."

"That's just swell," Bigley said glumly. "Guess I'm about to be called on the carpet."

Chan grinned.

"No need to worry—have visited impressive office of deputy chief, and no carpet lies on its floor. Only modest rug."

Bigley smiled weakly.

Taxi drivers frequented the block occupied by the hospital day and night in search of fares, but Bigley had found a spot nearby for the police department car he had requisitioned for Chan's visit.

"Just a few minutes' drive to the Hall of Justice," Bigley remarked, "so sit back and enjoy the sights."

The visiting detective looked with interest on the glimpses of the city afforded by the brief drive. As usual the walking public competed with automobiles—and both gave way when a trolley-car rattled by, its motorman shouting a warning to any unwary pedestrian courting disaster.

The driver knew his business, and the journey to Bryant Street was accomplished without incident. Within minutes of their arrival the two detectives were ushered into the deputy chief's office.

The red-faced Flannery was behind his desk, and he rose eagerly to greet them.

"Well, well—glad to see the two of you," the deputy chief said heartily. "Radio dispatcher informed me that you seem to be looking at two murders at that hospital, so I hope you have good news for me. How's your junior partner shaping up, Charlie?"

Bigley silently wished himself back on the beat, where encounters with deputy chiefs were rare.

"Detective Bigley has demonstrated qualities that point to future success in his career," Chan replied. "Progress in investigation and eventual solution will shine bright light on his efforts."

"Is that so!" Flannery cried. "Glad to hear it. I'll bet you thought I was going to chew you out," he told Bigley. "Not a bit of it. Charlie's too modest, of course, but that's his way. Success follows him like our famous fog after a sunny day, but he's always generous with the credit."

The phone on Flannery's desk interrupted his short spiel, and he picked up the receiver.

"Yes? Sure, send 'em in." Flannery hung up.

"Right on time," he announced. "Good thing you two were delayed at the hospital, since my other guests also phoned to say they would be a little late."

The door opened, and a man and woman in their mid-thirties entered. He was handsome, lean, sophisticated, yet casually dressed; she was clearly his equal: a striking, dark-eyed woman in professional garb.

Charlie Chan's face lit up at the sight of them.

"'Great is the joy of old men reunited with young friends,'" he beamed. "Ancient Chinese saying applies to present moment very well, I think."

Barry and June Kirk laughed, and shook hands enthusiastically with the detective.

"Same old Charlie," Barry Kirk said with a smile. "But your quote is a bit premature—you're hardly an old man just yet!"

"And we're not quite so young as we were when we first met," added his wife. "But Chinese philosophy aside, it's great to see you again."

Introductions followed, and the Kirks explained to Bigley how they had first encountered the detective from Hawaii. Years ago, the murder of Sir Frederic Bruce in Barry Kirk's penthouse apartment had been solved by the unlikely team of then-Captain Flannery, Chan and June, at the time an assistant district attorney. And June's early professional triumph was accompanied by a personal milestone when she became engaged to Kirk.

Chan assured the couple that his youngest son, Barry Chan, Kirk's namesake, was well.

"Handsome like original Barry," grinned Chan, "and inquisitive like father."

"I'm sure he inherited something from your wife as well," June Kirk put in.

"Hopefully, patience," Chan replied. "Mother of eleven children always sets example of forbearance and fortitude." The Kirks laughed appreciatively.

"Why don't you all have a seat," Flannery suggested, indicating his office conference table. "I don't want to interrupt the happy reunion, but we've got some police business to discuss.

"To begin with," the deputy chief continued after all were settled, "I think you all know that the contraband problem at the docks has been feeding the illegal drug trade here in a big way. I guess you'd say that I called in a favor when I asked Inspector Chan to take time away from his family including a new granddaughter to look into things, with our Detective Sergeant Bigley acting as his—not his assistant, more like a partner—"

"'Liaison,' perhaps, is best way to describe Detective Bigley's valuable role," suggested Chan. Flannery nodded, and went on.

"The two of them have had their hands full, and I wanted us to compare notes with Mrs. Kirk here, representing Mr. Hennessy—he's the U.S. attorney for California's northern district. June has been the deputy U.S. attorney in his San Francisco office for a number of years."

Flannery paused briefly.

"I don't mean to leave you out of the proceedings, Mr. Kirk, but—"

"That's quite all right," Barry Kirk said promptly. "I have no official standing and am happy to absent myself if you'd like—really I was just here to renew my acquaintance with Charlie."

"That's very gracious of you, but there's no need for you to leave the room," Flannery assured him. "You're certainly a solid citizen—a friend to the department," he said with the hint of a smile, "and I'm sure we can rely on Mrs. Kirk to keep you in line if need be.

"Now," Flannery cleared his throat. "June, why don't you start? After all, in the law enforcement pecking order Uncle Sam comes first."

All eyes turned toward the deputy U.S. attorney.

"Thanks, Tom," June Kirk said with a smile. "I'm glad to have this opportunity to compare notes with you and Charlie. Seems like old times, doesn't it?

"I won't give you chapter and verse of our office's continuing interest in this situation," she went on. "It's enough to say that we're seeing a great increase in activity across state and territorial lines, a real escalation in the kind of illegal drug trade that's been a concern for just about as long as anyone can remember—longer, even, since it dates back to the opium trade of fifty years ago or more."

"Like silver lining in dark cloud, great fire thirty years ago burned away many drug dens infesting Chinatown district," Chan remarked. "But descendants of evil always quick to invent new plagues that ruin many lives."

The attorney nodded.

"And the plague that we're fighting now is the continuing arrival of heroin in San Francisco," she said, "some of it bound for destinations elsewhere and much of it finding customers right here, and up and down the coast.

"That's why my boss has directed me to work with your department, Tom, and he's pleased that you've recruited Inspector Chan," said June Kirk. "Together we can put a serious dent in the flow of heroin into this port and put away some of the people responsible for a long time."

Deputy Chief Flannery had nodded several times in agreement during the woman's recital. Having overcome his reluctance to work with "a girl," as he had described June after their first meeting, he now had the greatest respect for her abilities.

"I know your time is valuable, Mrs. Kirk, so I'll save some of the details of the investigation so far," Flannery put in, "but I haven't told Charlie about the unusual tactic your office has undertaken. Since it's confidential and all, I thought I'd leave that to you."

"Pardon the interruption, please," Chan cut in, "even though murder investigation is a matter for police, not federal attorneys, important to point out that murdered *Monterey* crew member Notley was link to illegal drug trade.

"Quantity of heroin found in dead man's belongings before he was silenced in hospital bed by strangler, and short time ago body of hospital janitor found in same wing as unfortunate Notley."

"If Notley was in the middle of the contraband scheme," June Kirk frowned, "what about the second death?"

"Possible that janitor witnessed deed or knew killer," Chan replied, "but it seems certain that murderer who strikes twice in hospital with such ease has some connection to it. Familiarity with building needed to access patient's room, and only someone who frequents hospital hallways would know of janitor's closet where second body was found."

"Doctors, nurses, patients, visitors," mused Flannery. "That's a pretty big list of suspects, Charlie."

"Maybe with help of partner detective," Chan nodded at Bigley, "we can arrive at shorter list. But must apologize for delaying federal attorney from sharing confidential item."

"That's all right, Charlie," June Kirk replied. "You're correct—homicide isn't a matter for our office, but these deaths may lead you to the same solution we're pursuing from a completely different angle.

"What Deputy Chief Flannery was referring to—the unusual tactic our office has authorized—concerns a possible third place of interest. Some weeks ago," she continued, "one of our agents tracked a man suspected of involvement in illegal drug importation to a rather peculiar location. We don't know this man's name, he seems to use one alias after another and changes his appearance frequently as well. But we suspect he's at or near the top of the organization that's bringing drugs into the city on a grand scale."

The telephone on Flannery's desk rang, and he turned to answer it.

"Call for you, Charlie," said the deputy chief, handing Chan the receiver.

The conversation was brief. Chan spoke only a few words, hanging up in a few minutes. He turned to the group.

"Coroner confirms both victims strangled in same manner," the detective announced. "Examination of Notley's body revealed twin of mop strand found on floor of janitor's closet. Test results support my conclusion that the killer struck unlucky janitor first, then Notley."

Bigley opened his mouth to speak, but Flannery was quicker.

"How do you figure that, Charlie?"

"Dry strand left no trace of liquid on neck of janitor," Chan replied, "but on neck of unfortunate Notley laboratory tests discovered moisture and cleaning solution. When I examined closet crime scene, found dry strand used to kill Jenkins—but mop lying next to bucket of dirty water was wet."

All eyes were on the detective as he reconstructed the crime.

"After eliminating janitor, murderer employed mop in hallway as ruse to approach room of next victim, then entered room and pulled wet strand from mop to strangle Notley," Chan continued. "Leaving behind murder method in haste to depart, killer returned mop and bucket to closet before making escape."

Flannery nodded.

"Probably left the hospital the way he came in," he reasoned. "Somebody must've seen something, blast it. If we could just find a reliable—"

"Pardon, please," Chan interjected. "Telephone rudely interrupted most interesting narrative from federal prosecutor." He turned toward June Kirk. "You were telling of suspected drug smuggler who was followed by intrepid federal agent to strange place. Strange in what way, please?"

"I'll answer your question with another," she replied. "What career criminal would want to adopt a child?"

The group was silent for a moment. Chan appeared deep in thought.

"The suspect was trailed to a small private orphanage where adoption is the goal, and everything seems to be above board," she went on. "It's run by a woman named Lande who turned the family home she inherited into what she calls Homeplace Orphanage."

Charlie Chan stirred.

"The answer to your question is as clear as cloudless summer morning," he offered. "Man who practices crime goes to seemingly noble institution for some evil purpose, not to take charge of orphan. Perhaps someone at this orphanage knowingly or unknowingly provides false front for illegal activity."

"That's been our assumption all along, Mr. Chan, and it brings me to the last two points I wanted to make." June Kirk glanced at her watch. She and her husband rose.

"It's clear that the department and its temporary consultant have their hands full trying to figure out how two dead men connect to our bigger problem. In our office we have adopted the unusual tactic that the deputy chief mentioned, putting one of our people close to one of the smuggling route's key shipping points. The investigator in question has, shall we say, an extraordinary background."

She smiled at Charlie Chan.

"My boss calls this tactic a blessing in disguise. I think we can count on some success soon in that area.

"But we also need a look inside that orphanage," she continued. "Tom and I were talking about sending a couple posing as potential adoptive parents there—"

"Please excuse habitual rudeness," Chan interrupted. "Suggest that examination of organization's finances might prove interesting."

"I agree, Charlie," Kirk responded. "The operative I mentioned is focusing on that aspect of the case among others. In addition to following the money trail, the approach I'm thinking of would require two investigators to play the part of parents looking to adopt a child from the orphanage."

"I think that's a damned good idea," Flannery growled, "just not the couple you had in mind."

June Kirk smiled.

"I had volunteered myself and my intrepid spouse—"

"Who, me?" put in Barry Kirk with a laugh.

" —for this duty, but Tom objected."

Flannery reddened.

"Not that the two of you wouldn't do well in such a situation," he assured the Kirks, "but the fact is, you're both just a bit too well known in the Bay Area to go playing make-believe."

"I admit our—er—mugs have graced the pages of the better-known newspapers, separately and as a couple," Barry Kirk offered. "I don't know whether the not-so-nice people you're after read the society pages, but I agree with Deputy Chief Flannery. This mission calls for some less familiar faces."

As June Kirk nodded reluctantly, Charlie Chan broke in.

"Excuse this intrusion, but the notion has merit," he said, smiling. "This young couple, they must have their wits about them but appear none too bright—desperate for a child, they should seem open even to illegal arrangements. I have in mind a certain young man to play the part of the anxious husband.

"I speak of son Henry, who already possesses interest in this case and could seek information while playing the role of simple husband eager to please wife.

"It only remains, possibly," Chan proposed, "to find a suitable young woman—one who is intrepid and not so well known as locally famous attorney—to play the part of potential wife and mother."

The assistant U.S. attorney paused in the doorway. Chan's remark coincided with her train of thought.

"Your mention of Henry inspires me, Mr. Chan," June Kirk smiled. "Sometimes the best answer to a problem lies in plain sight, and I think between your son and the idea that's just occurred to me we may have the perfect couple."

Lily Wu enjoyed working in the new Federal Building, a recent addition to the city's so-called Civic Center district. The massive five-story grayish-white block was the latest of eight government buildings of California granite to rise from the ashes of 1906. On its third floor, in the offices of the U.S.

attorney for the district, Lily had found employment a few years ago in keeping with her law school studies. A petite, demure woman in her mid-twenties, her hair smoothly curled in the latest American fashion, she was the daughter of Chinese immigrants, making the transition from East to West like many of her generation.

In dress both professional and conservative she was indistinguishable from the many other young women who worked in the Federal Building where she served as a legal aide to the assistant U.S. attorney. Her fluency in English and Chinese—the Cantonese spoken by many immigrants in San Francisco—was a tremendous asset in the office, and her legal knowledge was growing apace.

It was at the university that she had first encountered fellow student of law Rose Chan not long before the latter's marriage to John Quincy Winterslip. The two young women had kept in touch as both struggled to balance law school, work and—in Rose's case—family.

Lily also knew that her boss, June Kirk, had encountered Charlie Chan early in her career, so the young woman wasn't surprised when the unorthodox assignment was offered to her. She was a determined young woman eager to take advantage of any professional opportunity that presented itself.

"I would very much like to—to do what you've described, Mrs. Kirk," she said enthusiastically. "It's very good of you to consider me for such a task."

"You're quite sure?" Kirk inquired. "I want you to mull this over carefully before accepting. We're dealing with some rather unsavory characters in this case, and it's unclear how or even if the orphanage connects to the smuggling of contraband.

"Also, there's still the matter of young Mr. Chan's willingness in the matter," she continued. "I'm fairly confident that he'll go along with his father's wishes, but this entire idea only arose for the first time last evening. Assuming he agrees, a little playacting should keep you safe if you both pretend to be, shall we say, more naive than average. At the same time it's vital that you go into this thing with your eyes and ears open."

Lily nodded.

"I think we should make a plausible couple in appearance. Rose—Mrs. Winterslip—has shown me family photographs, and Henry Chan looks like, that is to say—"

June Kirk was amused.

"A suitable pretend-husband?"

Lily blushed; discussing such topics with her boss was something new, indeed.

"What I was trying to say was that, together, we might appear to be any two people from somewhere between Broadway and Bush Street."

"That's one of the reasons I thought of you when Inspector Chan brought up the possibility that Henry would take this on," Kirk agreed. "The two of you look like a plausible young couple who grew up and met in Chinatown and are now intent on starting a family in the Bay Area."

A hint of mischief sparkled in her dark eyes.

"You'll just have to speak up quickly to keep Henry from displaying any tell-tale ignorance of San Francisco," she warned. "After all, his experience of the city is somewhat limited."

The two women laughed.

"With luck, we won't be subjected to an interrogation that requires in-depth knowledge of the Bay Area," Lily responded, grinning, "but I will recommend to Mr. Chan that he play the part of the strong young man of few words whenever questions concerning San Francisco come up."

Charlie Chan was the last to retire for the night at the Winterslip household. John Quincy had sleepily bade him goodnight while handing him the telephone. The instrument had managed only a half-ring before the lord of the manor snatched the receiver from its cradle to avoid disturbing other members of the family. Chan grasped the phone eagerly—he had been expecting a return call—and nodded his thanks to John Quincy.

"This is Charlie Chan speaking," he intoned formally. "Is that you, Miss Winget?"

The tinny voice came through clearly. Gertrude Winget was secretary to an administrator at the San Francisco university that figured prominently in one of Chan's investigations only a few years ago. She was fond of the detective, in her way, but she considered this a business matter; her tone was brisk and efficient.

"I've retrieved the information you requested, Mr. Chan. It's been several years since such a production occurred here, but I located our file and some other source material. I can summarize it if you like."

Chan grinned at the sound of the steely voice. There would be no small talk on this call.

"I am grateful for whatever information you can provide in response to my inquiry," the detective replied. "Thanking you in advance for same."

He listened intently as Miss Winget spoke rapidly, delivering her report without a pause. In less than a minute, she concluded with an open invitation to the detective to visit the campus in future whenever his professional schedule allowed.

Chan's smile broadened.

"It would give me great pleasure to renew our acquaintance at some future date," he said. "Perhaps at university theater production or other campus event that you enjoy."

Miss Winget thawed slightly in response, and the call ended with an exchange of pleasantries.

That night, Charlie Chan slept a dreamless sleep.

Chapter Seventeen

UNDERCOVER AGENTS

Breakfast in the Winterslip household was a quiet affair. Rose and the new arrival were still in the hospital, and the family matriarch was not an early riser. John Quincy had departed early for the office. "High time I put in an appearance before Roger finds he can do without me altogether," he quipped.

As father and son Chan shared a pot of tea and their impressions of the last few days' events, the detective broached the subject of "Mr. and Mrs. Huang" and their proposed visit to the orphanage. Henry was intrigued by the opportunity to take part in the investigation, however small his role, but wondered about involving a woman he had never met.

"Dad, you know I'm happy to help out, and I trust your judgment above all else," said Henry. "The only question I have is: Who's playing the part of my wife? I think we're going to need to talk this through—you, me and . . ."

"Young woman to be recruited by a trusted person in U.S. attorney's office, June Kirk," Chan replied. "You have heard me mention her as June Morrow in connection with the case of Sir Frederic Bruce. Perhaps the best way to proceed is to arrange a meeting to, as you put it, 'talk this through.'"

Stepping to the telephone the detective dialed the number of the federal building, and soon June Kirk was on the line.

"Charlie Chan speaks," the detective said cheerfully, "and a very good morning to you."

"Mr. Chan—good of you to call! Your timing is perfect," June Kirk said cheerily. "I've just recruited a wife for your son."

Chan grinned.

"So happy to hear that Henry has acquired a wife," he replied, eyeing his son. "Now young couple can begin to build a happy family by adding child to their household. Suggest we meet at your office, ten o'clock, to discuss plans for same?"

June Kirk answered in the affirmative and rang off. As Chan replaced the receiver in its cradle, he turned toward his son at the breakfast table only to find another family member close at hand.

"So!" Chan Chun Shee cried. "Henry has *wife*? What—when—" The matriarch of the Chan family had overheard just enough of her husband's telephone conversation to draw the wrong conclusion, and her ire burst forth in both English and her native language.

Chan and son were quick to calm the storm of outrage, and Mrs. Chan eventually accepted the terms of Henry's possible assignment.

"Please to make sure that when time comes for oldest son to make *real* marriage," she warned, "that you honor Chinese customs—not just American ways."

"You'll be the first to know, Mama," Henry promised.

The detective and his son arrived several minutes before the appointed meeting time and were shown into a small conference room on the third floor of the Federal Building.

No sooner had they sat down at the rectangular table than Detective Sergeant Bigley arrived, notebook in hand and flushed of face. "Good morning to you both," he said, breathing heavily. "I ran up the stairs in hopes of gettin' here early enough to give you the latest." He settled into one of the remaining chairs and patted his notebook with some satisfaction.

"I've been trying to track down anyone who might've seen something at the hospital," he explained, "especially the people in the waiting area and any hospital employees who were known to be on duty in that wing.

"It's a long list," he allowed, consulting his notes, "but I figure we have to start somewhere. That couple, f'rinstance. I ruled out the two people I noticed on my way to the telephone—you remember—one minute they were there, and a few minutes later they were gone? Harmless. They drove up from Soquel for the day to visit his elderly mother, and it all checked out.

"According to the nurse on duty," Bigley summarized, flipping through several pages of the notebook, "the rest of those waiting in that area during the time in question were regular customers. That is, the half-dozen or so persons other than the couple I mentioned were there for legit purposes and had been there the day before—and they were there the day after."

"What of hospital employees who were present in wing where two unlucky men met their end?" Chan inquired.

Bigley looked up from his notes.

"I'm still working on some of 'em, but the nurses are hard to get in touch with when they're not on duty," he answered. "As discussed, we still need to track down the second victim's boss—she's out of town, and I couldn't reach her by phone. And that," he said, closing the notebook, "is all I have at the moment—a bunch o' nothin'," he concluded ruefully.

"Detective work filled with small disappointments that lead to big results," Charlie Chan assured him. "Do not be discouraged."

"Good morning, gentlemen!" The men came to their feet quickly as June Kirk entered the conference room followed by Lily Wu. "I hope we haven't kept you waiting?"

"No inconvenience was suffered by us, and the wait was productive," Chan replied. "We arrive early to compare notes while anticipating arrival of legal ladies."

Kirk nodded, and presided over a round of introductions.

" . . . and I believe Lily already knows one member of the Chan family," she concluded.

"That's right," Lily Wu spoke up. "Rose and I were friends at the university," she said, looking at Charlie steadily. "She told me all about her family," she said shyly, glancing at Henry. "I'm very pleased to meet you.

"And you too, Detective Bigley," she added in a rush, anxious to make a good first impression.

Bigley and Charlie Chan nodded, and Chan was struck by Henry's expression. The detective thought that his son appeared just as he had on a scorching Oahu beach many years ago, when sunstroke had temporarily addled his wits.

The conference room was devoid of sunshine, Chan reflected wryly.

"Lily has agreed to take part in our scheme, and I believe young Mr. Chan is also willing?" June Kirk turned to Henry expectantly. There was a noticeable pause as he emerged slowly from the temporary befuddlement.

"Henry?" Chan senior said, nudging his son. "You have given sufficient thought to matter we discussed?"

Henry snapped to attention.

"Thought? Why, yes. But we only talked about it in general terms," he added lamely. "What, exactly, are we going to do—and when?"

"Excellent question," Kirk replied. "I have two answers for you. First, posing as a young married couple you can ask all manner of questions about the children in the orphanage's care—where they come from, the success of past adoptions, all that sort of thing.

"Second, you must improvise as the situation allows," she instructed the pair. "You may be able to overhear conversations, even get a look at some of the office paperwork.

"If this sounds like a fishing expedition that's because it is," the attorney declared. "Our investigation points to this place, but we don't know why. Our hope is that any suspicious activity happening under the guise of an orphanage will be hard to conceal from two sharp-witted persons actively looking for it."

"Remember to be open to impressions," Charlie Chan added. "Young woman who studies law and son of detective both equipped with brains capable of fierce thinking. Combine such with ancestral gift of intuition. You may discover a great deal or only a little, but small efforts can accomplish big things. Like Chinese proverb about man who moves mountain one small stone at a time."

June Kirk produced two pieces of paper and handed one to each of the fledgling undercover agents.

"This is a brief statement of who you two are supposed to be, your background and personalities. Just enough to give you a plausible appearance to anyone at the orphanage curious about your intentions."

"'Mr. and Mrs. Huang,'" Henry read from his copy of the document. "I see we're keeping our real first names?"

Kirk smiled.

"We thought it best, to avoid confusion," she confirmed. "I think the two most important things for you both to convey are your keen desire to adopt a child, preferably an infant, and your, shall we say, trusting, innocent personalities."

"What do you mean?" said Lily Wu.

"Permit interruption, please," Chan put in. "Attorney's careful language is always accurate, but policeman's blunt words are also sometimes helpful.

"Even an experienced investigator is sometimes tempted to demonstrate knowledge, but better that you two should pretend ignorance. The wise man plays the fool to catch the wary."

"I get it," Henry chimed in. "You want us to act like a couple of dumb-bells."

"Please!" Chan cried. "Unfortunate choice of words does no credit to Chan family—and you should regard Miss Wu with greater respect."

Henry reddened visibly and turned to his new "wife."

"Sorry, er, Lily—Miss Wu," he said quickly. "I didn't mean to imply—"

"Apology accepted," she said with a grin. "No offense was meant, and none was taken.

"I think I understand the distinction you're making, Mr. Chan," she said, turning to the detective. "We keep our heads on straight, pretend to be keen on adopting a little bundle of joy and act just a little bit more dimwitted than the average young man and wife might be."

"Excellent summary," Chan nodded approvingly. "Would only add emphasis on the need to cautiously explore opportunities that may arise—whatever they may be.

"Sometimes must cast long line to catch big fish."

Chapter Eighteen

DR. KLINDLEMAN'S BOOKCASE

Having charted one course of action in the investigation the group dispersed. The Kirks were bound for an official luncheon at which Barry Kirk planned to "play the role of dutiful spouse," as he put it. Detective Bigley was keen to continue his interviews of hospital personnel, and Chan indicated that he would soon follow the police detective.

"Please do not wait on me," he urged. "I will join you shortly after a few words with these newly wedded Huangs."

Charlie Chan and the newly christened Mr. and Mrs. Huang remained in the room. Commandeering the conference room phone "Mr. Huang" had no difficulty scheduling an afternoon appointment to visit the Homeplace Orphanage. The gears of their mission were now in motion, and Charlie Chan endeavored to impress upon the young couple the seriousness of their task.

"I will not repeat all that Mrs. Kirk said so eloquently," he began. "Henry has heard me offer words of caution many times and to repeat them now . . ."

He paused. Henry and Lily waited expectantly, respectfully.

"Play your roles as Miss Wu has described—like students slow to grasp lessons," he said emphatically. "Remain alert and hear all that is said to you, but keep to yourself any skepticism that arises.

"Thank you, Miss Wu, for agreeing to take on this most unusual assignment," the detective bowed. "Henry is fond of investigation. For him the matter might be a labor of love, but you have extended yourself beyond professional responsibilities, and we are grateful."

"You're quite welcome, Mr. Chan." Lily Wu glanced with interest at the red-faced younger Chan, whose thoughts were racing at his father's choice of words. *Labor of love, indeed!*

Having cautioned Henry and Lily, Charlie Chan departed for the hospital to join Detective Bigley as promised. He found the big detective pacing the hall between the two crime scenes.

"I've been up and down this corridor and talked to everybody I could find who was on duty or a patient earlier today, and no luck," Bigley said glumly. "And as far as I can tell, no patients from this wing have been discharged. Everybody who was here at the time of the murders is here now. If anyone *did* see anything, they're not talkin'."

"Low hanging fruit not always ripe," Chan assured him. "But it must still be considered before the harvester moves on to other possibilities.

"One other possibility remains to be explored," he went on. "Earlier we heard nurse mention top doctor of department where fatal misfortune strikes twice in one day, Dr. Klindleman."

"That's the one they call Dr. K.," said Bigley. "But I don't see how he would know—"

"Best to examine *all* fruit for ripeness," Chan grinned. "Even at the top of the tree."

The detectives were fortunate, Dr. Klindleman's secretary told them. He was just finishing a consultation and would be leaving the hospital for an appointment elsewhere in a few minutes.

"That's fine," Bigley replied. "A few minutes is all we'll need."

"You can wait in his office," the secretary offered. "He'll be in momentarily."

Dr. K.'s office bore all the hallmarks of a successful medical man including tasteful and expensive desk and furniture, two bookcases on one wall and evidence of extensive travel hanging on the opposite wall.

Chan scanned the titles on the bookcase. The shelves were crowded with standard medical reference works, such as Major's *Physical Diagnosis* and Clark Dudley's *Principles and Practice of Gynecology*, along with a large number of other medical works.

"*Statistical Methods with Special Reference to Biological Variation,* by Charles Benedict Davenport*," Bigley read from the spine of one hefty book. "Guaranteed to cure your insomnia or your money back. Also books by Dr. Freud, and a few with unpronounceable titles by a fellow called H.H. Laughlin. I'll bet his name isn't Hank! Find anything worth reading, Charlie?"

"Variety of works on medical sciences indicates keen intellect of a practitioner with passion for a newer branch of knowledge," Chan murmured, making a note of the book titles and authors. "Did your examination of office reveal anything of note?"

"Not that I could see. Photographs of places he's been to overseas—Japan, maybe, or China—somewhere over there. Certificates on the wall say he went to medical school, and he's a proud member of several fancy-sounding organizations," Bigley replied, reading off the organization names from framed documents hanging nearby.

"American Medical Association, American Association of the Advancement of Science, American Board of Obstetrics and Gynecology, American Eugenics Society, California Medical Association . . . This guy must be the real thing," the detective said. "What's that, Charlie?"

Chan had picked up a solid brass paperweight, a disc about the size of a silver dollar with a curious device on its face. He handed it to Bigley.

"Say, this would make a good weapon," the police detective quipped. "Some kind of diagram on the top of it—like two big commas. Looks foreign to me."

Chan nodded.

"Symbol is part of very old diagram called *taijitu* that represents ancient Chinese concepts of yin and yang," he said softly. "Unusual to see same outside of precincts of Chinatown—"

From outside the office an exchange of words between secretary and doctor announced Dr. K.'s arrival. Chan replaced the paperweight on the desk.

"Well, gentlemen," the well-known practitioner announced briskly as he entered the room, looking at a note in his hand. "I'm Dr. Klindleman, and my secretary tells me you're from the police department. How can I help you?"

"My name is Bigley, detective with the police department. This is Inspector Chan, on—er—temporary assignment here," J.P. began. The doctor nodded at Bigley and turned to face Charlie Chan.

"But surely—that is, I've seen you in one of our wards, haven't I? Ah, it was maternity, your daughter—"

Chan grinned and nodded.

"Happy to acknowledge earlier encounter with the skilled physician who escorted my grandchild into the world," he said. "Thank you for recalling this unmemorable face under less than pleasant circumstances, but present meeting unrelated to happy event earlier."

"Of course—you're here about the unfortunate men who were found dead?" Dr. K.'s brow furrowed. "Terrible business. I'm happy to answer your questions, but I'm not sure how I can help. I really know very little of the business, and I regret that I'll have to leave you soon for an appointment—"

"That's fine, doctor," Bigley assured him. "Just a few questions. I'm sure you know that one of the dead men was an employee of the hospital who worked mainly in your wing, according to what we've been told."

Dr. K. remained standing as though to reinforce that the interview would be short.

"Yes, so I've been told by the staff," he sighed. "These deaths—they've upset everyone here terribly, as I'm sure you can understand."

"Did you know either of the victims, Dr. Klindleman?"

The doctor's face betrayed no particular emotion, but Chan noticed a slight tic at the corner of his left eye.

"No," he replied. "Certainly not the boatman, the patient who was killed. As for the janitor, Jenkins . . . I'm sure I must've seen him at work, but we weren't on speaking terms."

"The hospital staff, you said that they were very upset since the deaths were discovered," said Bigley. "What about before—have there been any difficulties with employees or patients, anything unusual?"

Dr. K.'s gaze went from the police detective to Chan, who seemed more interested in the bookcase he had examined earlier than Bigley's questions.

"No, Detective Bigley, before these two horrible events nothing out of the ordinary had occurred—pardon me, Mr. Chan, did you have a question about my books?"

"Please excuse my curiosity, but have layman's interest in medical science," Chan said with a smile. "While we waited for your arrival, I took the great liberty of looking at weighty volumes on your shelves.

"You have acquired books for practice of medicine—or perhaps pursuit of research interest?"

The doctor smiled and stepped over to the bookcase.

"Was there a particular work that captured your interest?" Dr. K. inquired with a faint air of condescension. "Most of my collection would severely challenge the average reader, but I would gladly loan you anything you'd care to borrow."

"Very kind of you, thank you," Chan said. Quickly he selected three books: one by Davenport, two by Laughlin.

"I appreciate generous gesture," Chan said blandly, tucking the books under his arm. "Will endeavor to meet and overcome challenges presented by scholarly works."

"Very good," the doctor replied. "Now, if there are no further questions I really must be going."

Taking their cue, the detectives departed.

"Seems like the doc is top dog in his profession," Bigley remarked in the elevator. "All those fancy certificates, board memberships—"

"Excuse this interruption," Chan cut in, "but perhaps you noticed group photograph framed and hanging near diplomas?"

"Can't say as I did," the younger man admitted sheepishly. "I guess I missed it. What was it, Charlie?"

"Good doctor serves as member of many associations and societies," Chan noted. "Also on important organization boards, including Homeplace Orphanage. As Mrs. Kirk mentioned, that upstanding institution requires our attention because of possible link to smuggling of contraband.

"Strange coincidence," said the detective, "that eminent doctor who serves as orphanage trustee also practices his medical arts at hospital where two men die at hands of a killer."

"Him?" Bigley's eyebrows shot up as his voice cracked on the word. "That doctor? He may be a lot of things, but surely he's no killer!"

"Much to be determined," said Chan. "Maybe we learn more about medical man and workings of orphanage when Mr. and Mrs. Huang return from their meeting."

As he got behind the wheel of the sedan Bigley's mind was so focused on the many details of the case that he neglected to ask Chan about his sudden interest in medical science. For his part,

Charlie Chan was silent during their drive, already absorbed in a slim volume.

Braking to yield to a streetcar, Bigley glanced at his companion's reading matter. It was a book with a curious title.

Duration of the Several Mitotic Stages in the Dividing Root-Tip Cells of the Common Onion.

Buckley's brow furrowed.

Guess I shoulda stayed in school, he thought.

Chapter Nineteen

THEIR SECOND MEETING

In the downstairs parlor of Homeplace Orphanage the Huangs were well into their conversation with Virginia Lande. Henry was mystified. It seemed to him that the matron was treating them more like visiting dignitaries than prospective adoptive parents.

Tea was served, and the matron sat in a wing-backed chair facing the married couple seated on a wicker settee. They were every bit the picture of a recently married couple born and bred in San Francisco, and they were careful to present themselves as Kirk and Chan had recommended.

Miss Lande prided herself on sizing up potential clients from initial encounters, and her first impression of her guests was so positive that it opened a floodgate of possibilities which she rattled off enthusiastically.

"For couples such as yourselves—but only those truly dedicated to our work, mind you! —we offer several ways to support the children. You could adopt a child, of course. That's what brought you to us in the first place?"

Henry and Lily exchanged an uncertain glance.

"That's our eventual goal, certainly," Henry said with a catch in his voice. After clearing his throat, he remembered June Kirk's instructions.

"I think we need to hear more about the workings of the organization—where the children come from and how they have become part of successful families," said Henry, importantly.

"In short, stories of your success as an organization so that we can figure out how we might contribute to that success."

Lily saw an opening and took it.

"I agree with my husband," she said eagerly, nodding. "Before we consider such an important step, we need to know a great deal more about Homeplace. Our first impressions are wonderful, but—"

Virginia Lande smiled indulgently.

"Naturally you want to know all about us, and we in turn need to know more about you—as prospective parents, that is," she said smoothly. "As a first step, might I suggest—"

The ringing of a telephone just outside the parlor forestalled the woman's suggestion.

"Excuse me for a moment," Miss Lande said as she rose and walked toward the door. "I'm expecting rather an important call."

The orphanage head moved quickly, closing the door behind her. The telephone's ringing ceased, and the "Huangs" could hear muffled speech through the door. The exact words were unclear.

"How are we doing?" Henry whispered to his faux spouse.

"Fine, I think," she replied softly. "It seems odd that she wanted to talk right away about an adoption. I thought agencies were much more cautious in their approach, but she seems—"

The door opened, and Virginia Lande stood in the doorway with a troubled look on her face.

"I'm terribly sorry, but we'll have to postpone our conversation," she said apologetically. "That call—something urgent has come up quite unexpectedly, and I'll have to address it immediately."

The Huangs stood up and murmured words of regret and understanding, but Miss Lande interrupted.

"Yes, yes—very unfortunate, but I hope that we can continue this discussion soon. Would tomorrow morning do? I have no appointments before eleven."

"We'd be happy to return at ten tomorrow," Henry said quickly. "We have nothing on tomorrow morning, do we—dear?"

"No, indeed!" Lily chimed in. "We're just happy that you have the time to see us again."

"That's fine," the matron said, holding the parlor door wide. "I'll see you then, and thank you for your understanding."

The "Huangs" departed, but Miss Lande was not alone in the parlor for long.

A short time later she heard the front door open and close quietly. The parlor door opened, and Dr. Klindleman entered.

"I trust that my telephone call did not unduly disrupt your day?" Dr. K.'s inquiry was delivered indifferently, as if Miss Lande's day were his to disrupt.

"Just a bright young couple's visit, easily rescheduled," she replied. "Very likely they will end up adopting, but one never knows."

She paused for a moment.

"You have asked me in the past to make note of the apparent heritage of our parents and wards, so I should mention that this couple, a Mr. and Mrs. Huang—"

"Huang?" Klindleman's interest was evident. "Did you discuss their background at all?"

"There wasn't time," Miss Lande replied. "Your call—"

"Yes. We'll talk about that in a moment," the doctor said. "But this couple—'Huang' is a common family name in China. You don't know, I suppose—"

"Whether or not one or both of them is of Chinese ancestry? I can only say that they appeared to be," the orphanage matron said. "Certainly it's likely that their respective families hail from that part of the world, but they both spoke like well-educated Americans."

"No matter, no matter," Dr. K. murmured. "You say their visit will be rescheduled?"

"Already has been," she replied. "They're returning tomorrow morning."

"Possibly an answer to a prayer, if I were a devout man," Dr. Klindleman said abstractedly. "I beg your pardon—it's just that this couple might well prove to be the solution to the matter I wanted to see you about.

"But if they do agree to the proposal you will present to them we'll have to move quickly." He paused for a moment before continuing.

"For the good of the orphanage and its children."

The Huangs returned to their proper identities for the evening, and Henry reported their limited progress to his father at the Winterslip residence. John Quincy had just called from the hospital—with his mother-in-law adding commentary down the wire— to report that mother and child were to be discharged in two days' time.

Chan smiled as he hung up the receiver, delight shining in his face at news of the homecoming, then turned his attention to Henry's report of progress.

"It is encouraging that head of orphanage eagerly reschedules interested couple without delay," the detective noted. "You both must have made a positive first impression, and much may depend on second meeting. Remember to be alert for any opportunity to gather information, any chance to delve into workings of organization.

"Also," he added gravely, "take note of any mention of Dr. Klindleman's role with this orphanage."

"Rose's doctor?" said Henry, his interest piqued. The detective went on.

"Sometimes called 'Dr. K.,' physician who practices medicine at nearby hospital also serves on orphanage governing board," Chan explained.

"Not much time for digging up anything on him or anyone else today," Henry said with some regret. "We were only left alone for a minute or two when Miss Lande went to the phone. Maybe tomorrow will be different." He stifled a yawn; it had been a long day.

Chan patted his son on the shoulder.

"Sleep for the weary soothes like rain on parched earth," he said reassuringly. "Tomorrow will arrive with opportunities following behind—like wake that ship bestows on troubled waters."

Virginia Lande welcomed the Huangs to their second meeting as though they were old friends. Lily and Henry received the impression that for some reason they were now favored candidates for a deeper relationship with the orphanage, but as what? Adoptive parents? Prospective donors? Future board members?

Skipping the previous day's preliminaries Miss Lande resumed a version of the speech she had started to deliver then.

"To resume our discussion, let me begin by saying that if you're not yet ready to take on the commitment of adoption, as you indicated yesterday, a number of volunteer opportunities are available. Any of these would give you a better look at the inner workings of the organization.

"In fact there is something rather special that just might agree with your desire for involvement in the mission of Homeplace—not an adoption, but more of an exploration for those weighing that option against others."

She paused as if for dramatic effect.

"We do have an immediate need, an urgent need, for a married couple to perform a task that would require some travel."

"Travel?" Henry said with a note of skepticism. "To where?"

"That sounds wonderful," cried Mrs. Yuang. "My husband and I—well, the truth is we may not be quite ready to adopt, but we're really very keen on your work and want to learn more about it, to help in any way possible. The idea of doing something involving travel—"

Mr. Yuang picked up his cue.

"We'd be very interested in learning more about that," he affirmed. "Lily and I are happy to consider any such proposal you have for us. I know she feels just as I do, don't you dear?"

Mrs. Huang grasped Henry's hand and squeezed.

"Nothing would make me happier than to know we're doing something important for the children," she said eagerly, with a foolish expression perfectly performed for their audience of one.

The two exchanged a look tender enough to convince Virginia Lande.

"Well, then, why don't we discuss this matter further in my office?" Lande smiled at the young marrieds—*clearly very much in love, these two*, she thought tenderly. Setting aside her empty cup she rose to leave. The couple followed suit and walked, hand-in-hand out of the office and then single file up one flight to the second-floor office.

As they climbed the stairs Henry looked with interest at several photographs hanging on the stairwell wall. A few depicted children standing in small groups, apparently past or current charges of the orphanage. One or two photos seemed to be of new adoptive parents with their chosen son or daughter. In most of them Miss Lande was shown standing next to well-dressed people, individuals and couples.

"You'll notice pictures on the wall of the children with the new families the orphanage has made possible. Also you'll see photographs of some of our many volunteers and supporters, generous people who believe in what we do," the matron said over her shoulder as they neared the top of the stairs.

She's given this little speech a few hundred times, thought Lily, smiling brightly and murmuring approvingly.

Henry's gaze was drawn to a small photograph on the wall near the top of the stairs. Taking advantage of Miss Lande's continuing monologue, he lifted the framed picture from its moorings and slipped it into an inside pocket. Relief that the maneuver had escaped Miss Lande's notice caused him to stumble slightly on the top step, attracting a questioning look from Lily. He shook his head as they followed the matron into her small office.

"Please be seated." Miss Lande indicated the guest bench as she situated herself at the chair next to her desk.

"It's really and truly a blessing that the two of you came to see us," she told Henry and Lily. "We have had such a pressing need for a couple just like the two of you, a responsible husband and wife willing to undertake a trip on behalf of the orphanage.

"I realize that what I'm about to ask may seem rather unusual, but I can assure you that our innovative methods have had the best possible results," she went on vaguely.

"We also take every precaution to ensure that the child's needs, the little one's safety, is first. You would, of course, have to make certain guarantees to us—good faith assurances, legally binding, in writing, all that sort of thing. But if you are truly interested in our organization and advancing our work I'm sure that we can iron out all the details."

What on earth is she going on about? Henry wondered silently. *I guess this is the kind of thing Dad was thinking of when he said we should be open to any and all possibilities.*

"That sounds really intriguing," Lily said earnestly. "Please tell us more."

"You see, unlike our volunteer opportunities, the task that I'd ask you to take on would be, in effect, a temporary paid position—positions, I should say, since each of you would be paid. Your time commitment would be approximately two weeks."

"I'm due for at least two weeks off from work soon," Henry lied blithely, "so this would be a kind of working vacation for me. And Lily keeps house for us, so we're certainly available for this—er—assignment. You mentioned that travel is involved?"

Virginia Lande nodded, her face breaking into a broad smile.

"That's the best part of all," she cried. "You'll be paid to sail to and from Hawaii on board either the *Monterey* or the *Lurline*, depending on your scheduled departure date.

"Just think of it," the matron went on, sounding increasingly like a slightly dotty travel agent. "What an opportunity! Your expenses covered by our faithful donors, and generous compensation as well.

"Well! I've given you a lot to think about, I'm sure. Perhaps you'd like a few moments so you can discuss it privately," Miss Lande concluded. "If you agree then I have all the paperwork right here and we can settle the matter." She smiled genially.

"Let me just say that I look forward to standing on the pier and calling 'Bon voyage' to the three of you."

"The *three* of us?"

Lily's exclamation matched the startled expression on Henry's face. The matron tsk-tsked her chagrin.

"Oh, dear me! Where is my head today?" The woman raised a hand to her mouth in mock dismay.

"Why, the two of you—and the *baby*, of course!"

Chapter Twenty

THE STORM BROKE

John Patrick Bigley prided himself on what he considered excellent driving skills. The trip from San Francisco to Yountville, as he told his passenger, was accomplished in record time thanks to Bigley's willingness to exceed the speed limit. Charlie Chan smiled gamely in response, holding on to his hat (Bigley insisted the sedan's windows be left wide open) and, occasionally, placing both hands on what he often referred to as "the seat of all wisdom," his stomach.

Although the investigation was uppermost in their minds, Bigley did his best to act as tour guide for the visiting detective, noting the increasing prevalence of vineyards along the highway, and pointing out each growing village they motored through: Napa, Union, Salvador, Oak Knoll and, finally, Yountville.

Inwardly offering thanks to any listening deities for a safe arrival, Chan climbed out of the automobile and joined his enthusiastic driver as they walked toward the address Bigley had unearthed for Marjorie Crandall's sister.

Their destination was a faded gray bungalow situated on a slight rise, its large lot featuring front and back yards, both of them grassy and uncluttered. A lone shade tree dominated the front lawn. Although the street was quiet at the moment, neighboring families surely contributed to a livelier atmosphere at times since children's toys were evident in more than one nearby yard.

The faint rumble of thunder accompanied several large drops of rain as Bigley applied his knuckles to the front door.

The storm broke, and a windblown rain pelted the two men as Bigley knocked again. The police detective turned to Chan with a look of frustration.

"Hell of a thing if we drove an hour for nothin'—"

"Who is it?" a female voice demanded from within. "What do you want?"

"Police department," Bigley answered loudly through the closed door. "We want to speak to a Mrs. Baxter."

"Just a minute," the voice rasped. "I wasn't expecting company."

The rain and wind continued to dampen the two detectives, but in little more than a minute the door opened, slowly, and a gray-haired woman in a drab house dress peered inquiringly through steel-rimmed spectacles at the police detective.

"Yes? What is it?"

"Mrs. Baxter?

The woman nodded.

"That is my name. You said police—"

Out came Bigley's badge, produced from his hip pocket with the speed of a conjurer's trick.

"I'm Detective Sergeant Bigley of the San Francisco police, and this is Inspector Chan. We'd like to ask you a few questions. May we come in?"

The woman cast a glance over her shoulder, then shook her head regretfully.

"I suppose so—but you'll have to keep your voices down. My children are sleeping, and one of them is poorly. The doctor says it's probably the measles."

She stepped aside, holding the door wide for the two men's entrance and closing it behind them. The room's scant furnishings spoke of poverty and indifference to comfort, Bigley thought.

For both detectives, a glance was enough to survey the contents: a battered and faded blue settee, an old wooden rocking chair, and two occasional tables. A few threadbare rugs covered the dusty floor, and the walls were unadorned.

Mrs. Baxter was a woman of more than forty, the detectives noted, of less than average height and more than average weight. Bigley noted with some amusement her hastily applied makeup. *Poor old gal must not get out much, what with the two kids and all*, he thought. *She got gussied up in a hurry just for a couple of cops.*

"I hope this won't take long," the woman warned. "Have to keep an eye on the time so's I can give my little boy his medicine soon."

"Sorry to hear that he's sick," Bigley said sympathetically. "How old is he?"

"Eleven on his next birthday, which is coming up soon," the woman replied, the pride of a mother in her voice. "Just a year older than his little sister, and both of them a joy to behold—I wish you could meet them."

Chan looked at Bigley, who forged ahead.

"We were informed by her employer that your sister, Marjorie Crandall, visited you recently," the detective began.

"That's right. Marj was here for several days, helping look after the children," Mrs. Baxter said. "I wasn't altogether well at the time, and when I have these spells she comes and stays till I'm better."

Her expression softened.

"She's a treasure, the dear. It was just the two of us growing up, our mother doing her best after she was left high and dry," the woman said, sighing. "I suppose history does repeat itself, since my old man has been gone for a good many years now, and I'm following in my mother's footsteps, doing my best with two little ones.

"I have an advantage Ma didn't, though—a loyal sister. I guess you could say she's looked after me in one way or another ever since we were kids."

"Very commendable for a sibling to demonstrate such affection and commitment," Chan nodded. "You said she '*was* here'—her visit has come to an end, even though children are not all well?"

Mrs. Baxter appeared vexed, but only for a moment.

"Yes, I'm afraid she couldn't afford to take any more time away from her work," she conceded. "They're very understanding, the hospital people, but she can't take advantage of the situation—an older woman like her, she needs the job."

"Well, we would very much like to speak with your sister about some recent events at the hospital," Bigley put in impatiently. "Do you know how we can reach her?"

"Well, she has no telephone, but the best way to get a message to her is to call or send a wire to the hospital," the woman replied. "That's what I've always done.

"Of course," she suggested, "you could try the rooming house where she boards, I have the address if you'd—"

"No need, no need," Bigley cut in. "The hospital gave us that information.

"We appreciate your time, Mrs. Baxter. Charlie?"

He turned toward the other detective, whose face wore a thoughtful expression.

"You have been most helpful," said Chan, bowing slightly. "One more question, please. How long was your sister with you for her recent visit?"

The woman's hand was on the doorknob. She turned toward her questioner, frowning in concentration.

"Let me see now," she said deliberately. "It's hard to call these things to mind exactly. When you have youngsters, one day is so like another . . ."

Her expression brightened.

"Ah! She arrived on the twenty-sixth. I recall now, it was the same day I was able to go down to the fish man and buy something for our supper. If not for Marj I wouldn't have left the children on their own to run such an errand."

"And she left you to return to city and hospital work when, please?" Chan was penciling a few words in his pocket note-book, but he looked up at Mrs. Baxter frequently as he wrote.

"Just yesterday afternoon," the woman replied promptly. "The children and I were sorry to see her go, but no doubt we'll see her again soon—as soon as she can spare the time away from work, that is."

"Say! I have one more question," Bigley piped up. "How does your sister travel when she comes to visit? Does she drive her own car?"

"Oh, my—no, Marj has never learned to drive an automobile." She clearly found the idea of her sister behind the wheel of a car amusing.

"Well, then, how does she get here from the city?" Bigley demanded. "And how does she manage the return trip?"

"The trains are uncertain this far north, and that's a fact," Mrs. Baxter declared. "Each time she visits, it seems she makes a different arrangement. This time Marj mentioned begging a ride from some acquaintance or other—although I don't know whether she was referring to the trip here or how she was getting home."

She smiled affectionately.

"She's a great one for making her way in the world, and I ad-mire her for it."Again, the two detectives thanked the woman and made their way to Bigley's sedan. Mrs. Baxter stood on the porch and watched them go.

As the car pulled away from the curb, she waved goodbye.

Frustrated by the failure to track down the elusive cleaning matron, J.P. Bigley motored toward San Francisco faster than he had driven away from it earlier. Chan remained silent for several minutes, exploring a train of thought that was finally derailed by the automobile's encounter with a bump in the road.

"Wisdom arrives when haste departs," the detective noted, raising his voice to compete with the noise of the engine. "Perhaps we can compare notes and recover your good humor?"

Bigley laughed sheepishly, easing up on the accelerator and slowing the sedan to a pace more agreeable to Chan.

"Sorry, Inspector. I guess my frustration got the better of me," the police detective grinned. "It's just that we wasted all this time and still haven't talked to a woman who spends her days in that hospital wing. Seems as though she can give us a better picture of the situation there. In my experience, the folks who clean things up always seem to know what's goin' on."

"Having spent many youthful days cleaning big house, I can confirm your theory," Chan grinned. "However, today's trip to charming village was not a complete waste of time. People tell stories and sometimes places do, too."

"She sure talked a lot, and that's a fact," Bigley admitted.

Chan glanced at the younger man and thought of his own early forays into detection. Guidance from someone more experienced had been hard to come by then. Perhaps, he thought, some direction now would bear fruit later for this young man.

"At start of investigation," Chan began, "we know only that a crime has been committed. This one simple story of crime is like Chinese word *pu*, meaning wood in state of nature, uncarved. Each new story we hear cuts into this simplicity. The wood changes. Too many stories now distract from simple truth, like wood scarred by many cuts. We discard those to find simple solution that matches simple crime. Again we seek unblemished story, like *pu*, uncarved wood.

"Consider," he went on, "Asked about sister who works at hospital, helpful lady offers us interesting tale—unhappy childhood for her and her sister, dedication to her own children, sister's loyal support. House and yard tell their own stories also."

Bigley's eyes were on the road, but his mind was replaying the sights and sounds of their encounter with Mrs. Baxter. At length, he sighed in frustration.

"I know what you're saying, Charlie, but I'm not getting it," he lamented. "Maybe this case is too much too soon for a rookie like me."

"Let recent observations benefit from further thought," Chan urged him, "like seeds watered by spring rain. While you apply mental effort, please drive to police station house where I can make use of telephone. First, to call hospital in search of elusive cleaning matron as her sister so kindly suggested. Second, to determine whereabouts of Henry and Lily Wu and hear results of couple's visit to orphanage."

Bigley grunted affirmatively and cleared his throat preparatory to speaking, but Chan was not yet done.

"I would ask that you please visit once again the dwelling of Marjorie Crandall in San Francisco in case phone call to hospital fails to locate her."

"And if we can't find her," Bigley retorted, "what do we do then?"

"Patience lets the muddy water settle," Chan quoted softly, "until all becomes clear."

The younger man shook his head impatiently, grumbling under his breath. Chan turned in his seat and poked Bigley in the ribs playfully.

"Truth seldom can be reached as quickly as fast automobile can drive to San Francisco," the older detective said with a grin. "But maybe we reach destination in both instances—if you listen to aging colleague a little longer."

Chapter Twenty-One

BUNDLE OF TEMPORARY JOY

Mr. and Mrs. Huang left the Homeplace Orphanage in high spirits, having agreed to take charge of an infant bound for—Virginia Lande had assured them—a loving couple in Honolulu eager to adopt a newborn. It was, she admitted, an unorthodox method of placing a child so young for adoption.

"We always put the needs of the child, its future well-being, above all other considerations," Lande had said firmly. "I've devoted my life to these children, and our institution will do what's necessary—even bending the rules—when it will make all the difference in the world to even one child in need of a loving home."

Henry Chan had enjoyed playing the role of Mr. Huang and the opportunity it gave him to spend more time with Lily Wu, and the feeling was mutual. The two seemed to act the part of a loving couple with singular ease, and each of them was aware of a growing attraction—a realization they kept to themselves.

Discussing the matter at hand took up all their time, for now.

"Wow," Henry Chan exclaimed as they drove away in the borrowed Winterslip vehicle. "I guess we're in the soup now, for sure."

"'Wow' is as good a word as any," agreed Lily. "I know our instructions were to be open to anything, but really—"

"Somehow, I don't think Dad or Detective Bigley ever imagined us as instant parents, even for a week or so," Henry said wryly. "On the other hand, we couldn't very well say no and come away empty handed, so to speak."

"Well, Mr. Huang, we surely won't be empty handed when we become instant parents," said Lily with a laugh. "I don't know about you, but my experience with babies is limited. Nil, as a matter of fact."

Henry smiled broadly.

"Well, Mrs. Huang, I can give you suitable instruction as to diapers and other such necessaries when the time comes," he offered. "When a man is the oldest of eleven children, certain opportunities for experience present themselves. I can assure you that I took full advantage of those opportunities—sometimes unwillingly, I admit! Instant fatherhood for a brief time shouldn't be too difficult."

The time from agreement to action for "Mr. and Mrs. Huang" was short. They were to travel on the *Lurline*, a Matson liner scheduled to depart San Francisco for Honolulu via Los Angeles in less than forty-eight hours.

As Henry expected and to Lily Wu's surprise, Charlie Chan reacted calmly to news of their unusual venture—even to the substantial payments they were to receive, one at the beginning of the voyage and the second upon delivery of their "cargo."

"If suspicions prove correct, paying couple to transport newborn could be more than simply a strange departure from the typical adoption process," the detective told the couple in a last briefing before the voyage. "Much effort and money indicates greater criminal activity than possibly illegal adoption of single infant."

"Say, that reminds me," Henry exclaimed, reaching into his pocket and pulling out the small framed photograph he had taken from the orphanage.

"I swiped this when Mr. and Mrs. Huang visited Home-place. It was one of several photographs Miss Lande pointed out, mostly donors—but this looks like maybe a board meeting. I recognized two of the faces right away. There's the doctor, of course, but it's the other one that caught my eye—the Perkins fellow from the *Monterey*. You remember—I told you about him and his wife? That's him, I'm sure of it."

Henry pointed at the group photo, indicating one of the six men seated at a long table.

Charlie Chan looked long and hard at the picture. It was identical to the photograph in Dr. Klindleman's office that he had mentioned to Bigley. Next to Henry's shipboard acquaintance was Dr. Klindleman at the head of the table.

"Petty theft justified in this case," the detective said thoughtfully. "Portrait of your shipboard acquaintance provides valuable link between orphanage and—"

Chan stopped abruptly. Lily and Henry waited, but the detective was lost in thought.

"A link between the orphanage and what, Dad?"

"Connection to larger criminal scheme," Chan replied cryptically. "In a way, your presence on ship will provide bait with which authorities may secure evidence of same."

Henry Chan's enthusiasm was tempered by caution.

"I'm sure you're right, Dad," he agreed. "I just hope they spring the trap when the time comes."

"Before somebody eats the bait," Lily concluded.

The Huangs kept a decidedly low profile while making their travel preparations. Apart from packing enough clothing for two weeks' travel, the most significant preparation for the trip was a last stop before arriving at the pier—Homeplace Orphanage, where their bundle of temporary joy awaited.

At the dock the Huangs appeared to be a first-class couple smartly dressed for ocean travel. Lily wore a light-blue dress and matching halo-brimmed cloth hat that her office colleagues had complimented more than once, and Henry attempted to enter into the spirit of the proceedings.

In addition to his usual conservative dark suit with vest and snappy fedora, he had donned a pair of black-rimmed eyeglasses. He reasoned that the hat-and-glasses combination would alter his appearance enough to escape the attention of any casual acquaintance he might encounter, especially when it came time to dock at Honolulu.

Not that he was likely to run into anyone who knew him well, he reasoned, but it was important to be prepared for any eventuality. (And, he told himself, this would be his first investigative venture of importance.)

For obvious reasons, their low-key boarding was accomplished without any farewell from actual family or friends, but Mr. and Mrs. Huang enjoyed the emotional bon voyages directed at their fellow passengers. The couple and their new charge were soon settled in a suite booked for them by Miss Lande, who was absent from the dock despite her earlier enthusiasm about seeing them off.

The *Lurline* had cleared the harbor less than an hour ago. Light breezes swept the deck, and fleecy clouds scudded across a sky made golden by the late afternoon sun. It had been a fine day, but a dark blue haze in the western distance threatened worsening weather.

On an upper deck the Huang family was among passengers enjoying a promenade. "Mr. Huang" lit a cigarette as "Mrs. Huang" held the baby now in their keeping. The young couple exchanged nods and smiles with other passengers, whose casual acknowledgements warmed when they saw the weeks-old infant.

Henry Chan had just finished his cigarette and Lily Wu was trading pleasantries with a young mother who had stopped to admire the baby for a moment. As the appreciative woman moved on, Henry was surprised to see two familiar faces approaching.

Mr. and Mrs. Perkins, with whom he had passed the time aboard the *Monterey*. Unreasoning panic fought with the calmer side of Henry's nature as he quickly considered his limited options. Above all, he must avoid a lengthy conversation with a couple who knew him only as the unmarried and childless son of Charlie Chan. But how?

Turning his face toward the ship's railing and cupping his hands to light another cigarette, Henry tried to avoid eye contact with the Perkinses. Fortunately they were more interested in the baby than its "father." Mrs. Perkins expressed interest in Lily's new motherhood, asking a few typical questions that "Mrs. Huang" fielded as though she had been a mother for quite some time.

Tugging the brim of his hat down, Henry acknowledged the Perkinses with a curt nod and mumbled greeting that was lost in the wind and noise of the waves. He hoped that the hat and eyeglasses would be enough to avoid recognition.

"What a lovely little tyke," cooed Mrs. Perkins, bending over the bundled infant. "Looks just like you," she told Lily with a warm smile.

"Business takes us to Hawaii," Mr. Perkins added, "but we hope to start a family of our own someday."

Henry kept his back to the Perkinses, puffing nervously on his cigarette and looking down at the waves. *Pretend you're a sullen father still adjusting to his new responsibilities,* he told himself. *Maybe if you keep ignoring them, they'll grow tired of small talk and move along.*

"Come along, Cecily," Mr. Perkins said indulgently. "It's time we let these young folks enjoy their time with the little one."

Mrs. Perkins chucked the baby under its chin, and gave Lily a farewell smile as her husband took her arm.

"Thank you for stopping," Lily called to the couple as they resumed their stroll. Realizing that Henry was avoiding the Perkins couple for a reason, she waited a moment before turning toward him.

"Join me for a view of the ocean?" Mr. Huang said weakly without turning. He was taking no chances while Mr. and Mrs. Perkins were nearby, even if they were walking away.

"Henry, what is it?" Keeping her voice low Lily turned toward the rail, holding the baby in her arms.

"Can't very well enjoy an ocean voyage without taking in the magnificent sights and sounds of the Pacific, my dear," Henry assayed in his best Mr. Huang voice, that of the cheerful but none-too-bright young husband and father. "We'll always recall this first seagoing adventure as a family—"

A gentle tap on his shoulder sent Henry's heart into his throat.

"I beg your pardon, but I couldn't help noticing that you're a fellow smoker," a pleasant voice said. "Could I trouble you for a cigarette? I seem to have left mine in our cabin."

Henry Chan quailed inwardly at the sound of the innocuous words. Mr. Perkins had returned.

"Er—surely," Mr. Huang muttered in a hoarse rasp, Henry's attempt to speak in a voice as unlike his own as possible. He reached awkwardly into an inner jacket pocket, retrieving and extending a half-full pack—doing his best to keep his eyes averted in what he hoped was a natural manner.

"Thanks," the other man said easily, pulling a cigarette from the pack and putting it between his lips as he groped in vain for his lighter.

"Seems I left everything in my cabin," he said with a laugh. "So sorry to trouble you—could you provide a light as well?"

"Of course!" Henry reached into the vest pocket where he usually kept a small box of matches.

Empty.

"I—er—can't seem to find my matches," he stammered. "But surely—ah!"

He pulled a silver Ronson from his right hip pocket, one of the newer "wind-proof" lighters that he had bought just for his trip to San Francisco. A few flicks of his thumb produced a tiny teardrop-shaped flame.

Perkins leaned forward to ignite the cigarette, and Henry was forced to raise his head enough to ensure contact between the wavering little flame and its target.

Ignition achieved, Mr. Perkins drew gratefully on the cigarette and exhaled thoughtfully, his eyes narrowing. Mr. Huang dropped his gaze as he replaced the lighter, silently cursing his lost box of matches—he could've handed those over without risking eye contact—but maybe, he hoped, his features weren't all that memorable, maybe—"

"You!" Perkins hissed, stepping back two paces and startling his wife.

"What is it, dear—what's wrong?" Mrs. Perkins gasped.

"It's Henry Chan, the detective's son, that's what's wrong," her husband growled. "This whole thing is some kind of police stunt—"

"Henry Chan!" Mrs. Perkins snapped. "What the hell are you doing here, and who's this woman?"

"Never mind her," Mr. Perkins retorted through gritted teeth. "What are you doing with this baby, Mr. Chan?"

If Henry was temporarily at a loss for words, Lily was not.

"The baby is mine," she announced loudly. "This gentleman is escorting me, and—what business is it of yours? I'm going to call an officer if you don't leave us alone."

"Oh, no, my dear," Mr. Perkins rasped mockingly. "I think that we can settle this affair without involving anyone in a uniform."

Lily looked up and down the deck, but not a soul was in sight. No one had emerged from the row of cabins that faced the deck for quite some time.

"If you're thinking of raising your voice, think again," Perkins said abruptly, his hand disclosing a small snub-nosed automatic pistol. "And you, young Mr. Chan"—he gestured with the wicked-looking weapon—"will do exactly as I say. Stay right where you are, so that your wife can join you next to the rail.

"Remember," said the gunman, as Henry shifted his feet uncertainly. "One man's hero is another man's dead fool."

An infant's cry joined the tense conversation. Perkins turned his attention to Lily, who was cradling the baby in her arms.

"You—hand the little tot over to Mrs. Perkins and then join your husband for a closer look at the ocean. No arguments!"

Lily complied reluctantly. Mrs. Perkins clutched the infant and moved to her husband's side.

"Now, then," Perkins said tersely. "I won't shoot you unless I have to. Just climb onto the railing, both of you, and swing your legs over the side so you can sit on the top rail . . . that's it, that's it . . . not very comfortable seating, but don't worry. You won't be there long."

Henry and Lily had slowly followed directions, seating themselves unsteadily atop the railing, each of them gripping it desperately with both hands.

"It will be so sad when Mrs. Perkins and I have to report that the two of you decided you couldn't face the responsibilities of parenting and decided to end it all in this dramatic fashion," he said mockingly.

"'She seemed quite unstable,' I'll say. 'Poor Mr.—Huang, was that his name? He couldn't bear her unhappiness.'"

"'She gave me the child to hold, but of course we had no notion that they would do away with themselves,'" Mrs. Perkins chimed in, reciting her lines with the sincerity of an actress in a melodrama.

The Perkins nodded at each other approvingly as though they were looking forward to their performance for the captain or some other ship's officer.

"Who knows?" said Mrs. Perkins carelessly. "If you're very strong swimmers, you might stand a fighting chance of being picked up by some wayward vessel. Although," she added casually, "I've heard it said that sharks frequent these waters in great numbers."

"Enough of this!" snapped the gunman. "I'll do the honors, and both of you keep your hands on the rail or—"

"One moment, please!"

Charlie Chan, gun in hand, stood in the doorway of the nearest cabin.

"Be so kind as to lower pistol, Mr. Perkins," the detective cried. "'Police stunt' is over, and I would be filled with grief should demonstration of my marksmanship become necessary."

Chapter Twenty-Two

PRISONER IN THE BRIG

T he gunman's eyes narrowed, darting back and forth. "It appears that we have each other at a mutual disadvantage, Mr. Chan," he shouted above the noise of the ocean. "I think you would rather not lose one of your many children, so why don't you put your gun on the deck and walk slowly toward me."

"To paraphrase famous book of etiquette," Chan replied loudly, "the disadvantage is all yours. Please allow me to introduce Detective Bigley of San Francisco police, who points a revolver toward your back at this moment."

"Two against one, Perkins," J.P. Bigley shouted with a note of triumph in his voice. The detective and the barrel of his police revolver jutted from an open porthole overlooking the promenade deck. "Better do as Mr. Chan says."

Perkins cursed and flung the gun over the side.

"My wife and I have done nothing except intercede on behalf of the Homeplace Orphanage," he seethed. "Some kind of fraud is being perpetrated here, involving your son and his female companion. They've taken this child, this infant, unlawfully," he blustered, warming to his chosen line of argument. "As a member of the orphanage's governing board, I challenged the two of them and my wife has taken charge of the baby."

"Board members of charitable organization always use firearms to fulfill their duty?" Chan said crisply. "Or maybe weapon was issued to you by Our Lady of Troubled Pilgrims Sacred Order before you boarded Pan American Clipper—

"—Sister Clarice."

Detective Bigley had emerged from the cabin where he had hidden in time to hear Chan's challenge to Perkins.

"Say!" Bigley quipped. "I know the sisters can be strict, but a nun with a gun? That's a new one on me." The detective approached the group, keeping his weapon leveled at Perkins.

With the threat of gunplay gone Chan pocketed his automatic and addressed Perkins.

"Clever actor who impersonated religious woman performed excellently," the detective conceded, "and flowing garment provided ample room for contraband. Consider," he addressed Bigley and the Huangs, "what customs agent would suspect woman of faith dressed in religious uniform of smuggling?"

"That's a very fine story, Mr. Chan," Perkins sneered. "I'm sure a jury would find it amusing, at best. You have no evidence! Do I look as though I could pass for a woman—let alone a nun?"

"Two mistakes helped pierce your disguise," said Chan, ignoring his quarry's outburst. "Things no actual nun would do.

"First, long overnight journey on Clipper presented problem to man posing as woman—how to hide growth of facial hair over many hours. You chose to conceal tiny hairs with pale makeup that could be applied even in darkness, a task easily accomplished by one with your theatrical abilities."

Chan paused, but only for a moment.

"Perhaps unfamiliar with dictates of religious orders, you did not know that real nuns do not use cosmetics. On Clipper, I was at first amused that nun wore 'paint and powder,' as some call it, but your second mistake indicated that made-up nun was no laughing matter."

"And what was this second mistake?" scoffed Perkins, whose normally pale face had taken on a ghastly hue.

"Again, ignorance led you to make fatal error in consuming delicious morning meal offered to all passengers," Chan went on relentlessly. "Those in holy orders fast on Fridays—and avoid meat as well. Passengers on Clipper boarded plane on Thursday evening, and broke their fast on Friday.

"Nun that wears makeup and ignores rules of her order—these two clues landed with a great thud on foolish detective slow to detect disguise of guilty man."

In a flash Perkins grabbed the infant from his wife and turned to the ship's railing, dangling the baby over the rail.

"Stop where you are," he commanded. "Put that gun down, you."

Bigley's revolver wavered. He hesitated then turned to Chan, who nodded. Slowly, Bigley put the weapon on the deck and kicked it toward Perkins.

"Keep your hands away from your pockets, Mr. Chan," snarled the miscreant. "Especially the one where you put the pistol. Now, back away—all of you."

"Melvin!" Mrs. Perkins shrieked. "Think what you're doing!"

Bigley and the others hesitated, reluctant to move in any direction. Charlie Chan stood his ground, addressing Perkins.

"Strongly suggest you consider consequences of threatened action," he warned. "Charges enough may be lodged against you—why condemn yourself before witnesses with additional crime?"

"Shut up!" Perkins shouted. "No more talk! Step away now, both of you, or you'll wish—"

Too late the desperate man realized that he had all but ignored a two-fold threat. In an instant Henry tackled the baby's captor and Lily wrapped the infant in a protective embrace, falling to one side as the two men struggled. Bigley moved quickly, retrieving his revolver and pressing its snub nose against Perkins's temple.

"That's all, Perkins," growled the detective. "Hold still or I might be tempted to spare the court a whole lot of trouble."

The tactic worked. Perkins slumped to the deck, and Bigley placed handcuffs on his wrists, pulling the arrestee to his feet.

"All right, all right," the prisoner said quietly. "Let me stand on my own."

As Perkins got to his feet, his expression was defiant.

"Just what am I accused of," he snarled, "besides holding a baby carelessly?"

Charlie Chan stepped forward, a look of well-deserved triumph shining brightly in his eyes.

"List of charges will be long," he said matter-of-factly. "Murder, kidnapping, trafficking in illegal drugs—"

"Prove it!" Perkins hissed. "You can't charge me with smuggling something that hasn't been smuggled, drugs in some hypothetical container in Hawaii."

Chan turned a stern face toward the handcuffed man.

"Your confederates at other end of smuggling route already in custody," he announced. "Wire from Honolulu police received by captain of this ship confirms there has already been much talk from those under arrest. They have agreed to testify against you and the woman you call your wife."

Perkins straightened up, looking Bigley full in the face.

"That—what you said about sparing the court trouble?" said the prisoner.

"Yeah?"

"Seems like a good idea," Perkins said through gritted teeth.

With a deft movement, the handcuffed man jackknifed backward over the ship's railing.

The crew of the *Lurline* responded to shouts of "Man overboard!" from Henry Chan and Detective Bigley. In short order the ship reversed course, and search-and-rescue efforts were underway.

Bigley had taken the distraught Mrs. Perkins into custody while Charlie Chan visited the bridge to request that the captain signal a police launch waiting to rendezvous with the *Lurline*. With their prisoner in the brig, the two detectives took Henry and Lily to the crew's mess to wait for their ship home to arrive.

"The cook figured we might want something to drink," Bigley announced, setting a tray with four mugs of coffee on the table before them. "He just made a fresh pot."

As the four savored the hot coffee, Charlie Chan explained the impending arrival of the police launch to Henry and Lily.

"When Detective Bigley and I planned brief cruise on *Lurline*, we anticipated possibility of return trip to San Francisco with or without guilty parties," said Chan. "Deputy Chief Flannery kindly arranged for his department to provide transportation if need arose not far from harbor."

"I wondered why you were so quiet about our upcoming—er—mission," Henry remarked, "but why didn't you tell me that the two of you would be keeping an eye on us?"

"Better to keep secret the necessary arrangements and remain hidden until guilty parties revealed themselves," his father replied. "Also, it was felt that both of you would be more convincing as foundling's parents—alone and helpless—to make you attractive targets for—"

"I get it," Henry interrupted. "We were bait, and we had to look and act the part."

His father nodded, smiling.

"I surely felt like bait," Lily Wu chimed in. "Like a fly in a spider's web."

"Please accept my apologies, Miss Wu, but it was necessary to place the three of you in harm's way—even though we were nearby to lend assistance," Chan said. "Police decided best way to trap the guilty was to involve the innocent. Sincerely hope that the experience will not result in nightmares for you, or fear of future ocean travel."

The former Mrs. Huang smiled gratefully.

"Thank you for your concern, Mr. Chan," she replied. "No permanent damage was done, but I am glad that it's over."

Detective Bigley blew on his coffee to cool it and lit a cigarette.

"According to scuttlebutt from the galley crew the search efforts are over. Mr. Perkins definitely won't be joining us for the trip back to San Francisco," he reported. "The district attorney likes live murderers better than dead ones, but I guess Mrs. Perkins can be charged as an accessory—and that will be that."

Charlie Chan's eyebrows rose over the top of his mug as he sipped from it.

"As polite English gentlemen say, 'I beg to differ,'" Chan countered. "'That' will not 'be that' until our journey is completed."

"You mean it's not?" Bigley spluttered, spraying drops of coffee onto the table. "But I thought that Perkins—"

"We have traveled far in short time," Chan replied, "but the last mile of a long trip is the most important of all.

"Mr. Perkins took part in smuggling scheme much bigger than work of one man, or two persons," he continued, "but he was only one of several who carried out instructions. He was not boss of operation.

"And he was not murderer."

For several seconds no one spoke as Chan's words sank in. Finally, Henry ended the silence.

"If not Perkins then who—who's pulling the strings, and who killed those two men in the hospital?"

Chan smiled.

"If my suspicions prove true, then your well-chosen words are doubly meaningful," he said thoughtfully. "Have already sent radiogram to Deputy Chief Flannery asking that he prepare for meeting of interested parties.

"Once we arrive at dock, police escort will speed us to Hall of Justice," said Chan.

"Perhaps there we can walk last mile together and arrive at truth."

Chapter Twenty-Three

THE LAST MILE

B etter than the escort Charlie Chan predicted, two patrol cars with drivers were waiting for the police launch to dock so they could speedily transport Chan father and son, Lily Wu, Detective Bigley and Mrs. Perkins to Tom Flannery's conference room.

Sirens and lights heralded the small procession's approach to the corner of Kearny and Washington Streets, a location for many things over the years—gambling hall, saloon, theater—where now the gray and solemn Hall of Justice faced Portsmouth Plaza.

Bigley, Chan and their entourage made their way to Flannery's office, and his secretary soon situated them at the deputy chief's long wooden conference table.

They had just taken seats when Flannery's voice boomed from the hallway. The door opened, and the red-faced deputy chief ushered in three additional participants in the proceedings.

"Hello again, Charlie!" cried June Kirk. "And Mr. and Mrs. Huang! So glad that you two were able to enjoy your brief marriage and an even shorter honeymoon voyage," the deputy U.S. attorney said with a smile.

"Now, Mrs. Kirk, this is a joint investigation with lots of moving parts, and I'm not going to pretend that our men on the force have handled it alone," Flannery began, "so I want you to conduct this meeting anyway you see fit. I think

Detective Bigley and Inspector Chan will be able to provide several of the missing pieces, too," the big man grinned. "So, June—the floor is yours."

"Thanks, Tom." June Kirk and the two other late arrivals took seats at the long rectangular meeting table. "I think a few introductions are in order. I'm June Kirk, assistant U.S. attorney for this district of the state."

Kirk turned toward a distinguished looking man seated next to her, a familiar face to Henry and Lily.

"I think some of you know Dr. Klindleman, the obstetrician. I would add that he's here today not as a medical man, but in his capacity as the chairman of the board for the Homeplace Orphanage."

Dr. K. was well known, and there was a murmur of acknowledgment around the table. Recognizing Charlie Chan, the doctor nodded at the new grandfather in a friendly manner. Chan bowed slightly in return.

Last of all her introductions, Kirk indicated Nurse Meadows, next to Dr. Klindleman, and a demure, dark-skinned woman seated at the far end of the conference table. She was in her late twenties, dressed in the professional garb of an office worker.

"Let me introduce to you the operative from our office who's been very much involved in the investigation—in a rather unusual way," June Kirk announced. "This is Durah Osogo."

A curious expression came to Chan's face. He realized where he had seen this woman before.

Durah Osogo greeted the assemblage in the lilting English prevalent in the British territory of east Africa, and Kirk continued.

"Miss Osogo is not only unknown to all of you, but she has remained unknown to almost everyone in my office—even though she has been involved in one aspect of this investigation for several months.

"As Deputy Chief Flannery knows, we've been aware for some time of the increased flow of contraband, most of it illegal drugs, transported from Honolulu into San Francisco for local and wider distribution. Flannery's men, the customs officers, our office—we've all been working together to determine where the big shipments come from, their point of distribution here, and perhaps the biggest question of all: Who's in charge?"

Everyone at the table listened intently. Only Mrs. Perkins appeared distracted, occasionally dabbing tearful eyes with a handkerchief clasped in handcuffed hands.

"Not that we've been idle along the way," Flannery put in with a hint of his usual bluster. "With the help of some of our federal friends we raided Calico Jim's and the warehouse behind it where the drugs were being stored and distributed. We're questioning Jimmy Moran. Seems pretty clear he was fronting for the gang's work on shore, but it may be that he was leaning toward Notley's point of view—that it was time to blow the whistle on the whole thing."

The deputy chief nodded toward Chan.

"That setup struck the informant I mentioned to Charlie as a kind of joke, and it was on his mind when he told our officer, 'old bootlegger new shebeen,'" Flannery explained. "Moran was a well-known bootlegger in the Prohibition days, running his 'soda parlor,' and now the old bootlegger was running a 'new shebeen'—but one that sold drugs instead of booze.

"The steward from the *Monterey*, Craxton, he's cooperating," the deputy chief went on. "All in all the boys have caught a good many small fry, but when we ask them about the big fish, they all clam up."

"Spoken like an avid fisherman," Kirk said with a laugh. "Tom, there's no question your department did everything possible, and you and I came to the same conclusion. We needed to pool our resources and ask Inspector Chan to join us.

"Charlie, I think I'd like you to take a turn in telling this story," she said. "I've got a few items that may come in handy, and those can be added as we go along."

The detective from Honolulu stood, bowed graciously, and began to walk to and fro near the head of the table, like a professor delivering a lecture.

"In any investigation," he began, "police draw on experience as they look to solve each new puzzle.

"Example of old opium ring case in Honolulu provided starting point for rumination while I recently traveled on Clipper. In past case smugglers shipped large quantities of raw opium from one port to another, and oceangoing vessels were their only option.

"But now, as told to me by my chief and San Francisco police, criminals seek to transport drugs in powdered forms—morphine, heroin—and modern progress has provided new means of smuggling. Ships can still be used, but another option presents itself.

"While in Clipper high above ocean, this foolish detective discovers he is flying in giant potential clue."

Chan grinned at his listeners.

"Consider," he said to the small, rapt audience, "that airplane able to transport stout Chinese traveler thousands of miles could also contain contraband concealed in clothing, on person, in luggage.

"Innovation is sometimes mother of transgression," he continued.

"Remarkable introduction of travel by air over great distances is still so new for illegal purposes that police only now are discovering clever smuggling methods."

"But Dad, are you saying Notley's shipboard stuff"—Chan raised an eyebrow at one of Henry's favorite slang words—"was just some kind of diversion?"

"Criminal organization demonstrated great ingenuity by shipping contraband in multiple ways, thus ensuring that at least some would escape attention of authorities," Chan countered.

"And some involved in scheme were themselves users of deadly product. The unfortunate Notley involved himself in smuggling aboard *Monterey*, but he grew fearful and made plans to betray others in the organization. Perhaps he regretted involvement and thought conversation with son Henry would provide path to reporting contraband operation to authorities.

"Some questions still to be answered," he acknowledged, "but continued questioning of crew and acquaintances of seagoing man will reveal truth—that Notley's descent into waters of harbor was no accident."

"That wire from your chief this morning," Flannery cut in. "It really fills in some of those details—"

"Excuse my rudeness," Chan interrupted. "Will share that information in due course, but Chief's contributions to investigation should remain known only to police, for the present."

"Whatever you say, Charlie," Flannery said magnanimously, his florid face turning one shade redder. "Please—go on with your story."

Chan paused his pacing and bowed slightly.

"Thank you so much."

Mrs. Perkins's occasional sniffling was the only sound in the room. All eyes were on Charlie Chan.

"Suspicion that nuns were impostors gave traveling detective excellent reason to examine others on Clipper, and prompted request for the capable San Francisco police department to search records for all names on passenger manifest." Chan nodded at Flannery.

"Police research found that all those traveling with me on flying boat 'checked out ok,' as son Henry would say," the detective noted. "All except three: a woman called Mrs. Claude Parker, and two members of sacred order of nuns.

"Also asked police to look for paper trail related to married couple named Perkins who traveled aboard the *Monterey* recently with son Henry," said Chan. "Strange that the man and wife known as Melvin and Cecily Perkins exist only in ship's record of that voyage and in publicity related to Homeplace Orphanage.

"Photograph obtained by son Henry shows Mr. Perkins—whose face bears remarkable resemblance to Sister Clarice, so-called nun who ate hearty but sinful breakfast with me on Clipper."

"That's absurd," exclaimed Mrs. Perkins tearfully. "My Melvin would never wear women's clothing, and he certainly wouldn't pretend to be a nun."

"Husband's decision to take his own life served as confession, Mrs. Perkins," Chan pointed out, "but please be patient—your turn in this story will come.

"Many hours spent on flying boat gave me ample time to study fellow passengers," the detective continued. "Mr. Perkins—Sister Clarice—was not the only person attempting disguise.

"Sister Margareta, who spoke very little English, also violated holy dietary rules of order—eating on Friday, and consuming meat at breakfast."

Chan smiled at June Kirk—and her special investigator, Durah Osogo.

"Miss Osogo's English today much improved since she wore religious uniform of Sister Margareta," he remarked. "No doubt undercover investigator learned much about secretive activities of those conducting drug smuggling."

June Kirk laughed, and Miss Osogo permitted herself a modest smile.

"It was thought that I could learn more by speaking hardly at all and listening a great deal," she explained. "It's surprising how freely people talk when they think you know very little of their language.

"The details will be in my report to Mrs. Kirk," said Miss Osogo, "but I can confirm that this man called Melvin Perkins—we're still trying to establish his true identity—managed to masquerade quite successfully as Sister Clarice. The disguise was a useful way for him to smuggle contraband and conduct—er—a number of other illegal activities. And the nature of the order's work allowed him to be absent for long periods of time without question.

"As for the, ah, activity at the orphanage, Inspector Chan," she continued, "I did my best to point you toward Homeplace without arousing suspicion in my . . . fellow nun. The more I learned, the more I was certain that you could find the connection between the hospital and the orphanage." Again, she smiled modestly. "Saying 'place-home' was as close as I dared go, and I had to make the effort—I wasn't sure if I would have the opportunity again."

Chan nodded and returned to his summing up.

"On passenger manifest, police found third name that was an alias, 'Mrs. Claude Parker,' " the detective said calmly. "She was a quiet woman for much of flight, eager to escape attention of fellow travelers—especially watchful eyes of detective. But when night fell, woman called Mrs. Parker could not resist whispered conversation with her husband.""Her husband?" Bigley's eyes widened.

"You did not realize that your words were overheard, did you—" Chan turned to the tearful Mrs. Perkins—"Mrs. Parker?"

Clutching her handkerchief, the woman glared at the detective but said nothing.

"First on board *Monterey* you impressed son Henry by playing role of Mrs. Perkins with so-called Mr. Perkins at your side. Later Henry mentioned to me how your husband was thin and you were stout—like nursery rhyme—and it occurred to me that supposedly stout woman might easily conceal small packages of drugs on her person.

"At end of voyage you and he completed your contra-band smuggling task and quickly returned to Honolulu to continue criminal enterprise. To evade scrutiny of author-ities, you assumed disguises to transport still more illegal drugs on Clipper flight to San Francisco—too many com-ings and goings of same couple would attract unwanted attention. But who questions a nun?"

All eyes were on Charlie Chan. The woman glared at him but remained tight-lipped.

"Again posing as stout woman you concealed contra-band on person, just as husband hid drug packages under nun's tunic."

Flannery's mouth had hung open for several seconds. Now it closed with a snap.

"Great Scott, Charlie! This is a hell of a story you're telling, but how could these two pull off all this playact-ing?"

In answer, Chan pulled a yellowed rectangle of folded paper from his pocket.

"Finding handbill in unfortunate Notley's bunk provid-ed some direction," he explained. "Promotional language indicated long-ago performance occurred on campus of well-known San Francisco university, so I sought additional information from old friend there," he continued, unfold-ing the paper. "This Notley once studied at same institu-tion and became acquainted with two actors in traveling company shown in handbill photograph."

The detective pointed carefully at two faces among the cast, both dressed as women.

"As cousin Willie Chan would say, I 'hit jackpot' in ques-tioning long-time university employee. She recalled student Notley as eager theater volunteer who sought to meet and befriend members of cast, especially the two known to us as Mr. and Mrs. Perkins.

"Conversation with university acquaintance also enlightened detective ignorant of main plot device used in play called 'Charley's Aunt.'"

Flannery's mouth was closed, but his expression remained puzzled. June Kirk broke the silence.

"Of course! A play where a man plays the part of a woman—"

"And in long-ago production that part was played by man we know as Mr. Perkins, also nun on board Clipper," Chan interjected. "He and Mrs. Perkins, also pictured, began criminal activities while in touring company. They cultivated young, impressionable Notley—leading to more recent criminal partnership involving smuggling of contraband."

"But what about the numbers on the other side of that handbill?" Henry Chan piped up. "And the two boxes, or whatever they are?"

"Unfortunate Notley alone knows answers to those questions," Chan admitted, "but possibly he was comparing his share of profits from drug sales to total—to see if he and two partners would receive equal shares.

"Two boxes may have been idle drawing of tavern called Calico Jim's and adjacent warehouse behind it," he continued. "Both math problem and sketch remained unfinished, perhaps Notley was at work on same when he was called on deck to meet his unfortunate end."

Flannery took a deep breath and exhaled noisily.

"Say, how many more names does this Perkins-Parker woman have?" he demanded.

"Maybe many," Chan admitted, "but only one more that concerns us here today.

"I think greatest role was character you created to identify unfortunate women and their offspring—name you adopted so you could come and go freely from hospital."

Chan looked around the table at the expectant faces before returning his gaze to the woman of many names.

"First you were Mrs. Perkins, then Mrs. Parker," the detective said solemnly, "but you are also Marjorie Crandall.

"*You* are murderer."

Chapter Twenty-Four

THE MASKS FALL

S ilence filled the room for a few seconds as Chan and the woman he had accused gazed at each other.

J.P. Bigley looked first at the woman, then at Chan. The police detective's face was a study in skepticism.

"Hold on now, Charlie. This woman—Mrs. Perkins—she used another name while traveling on the Clipper so she could help her husband move the contraband—that makes sense. But now you're saying she was that old dame Crandall, the hospital cleaning matron—*and* the murderer?" Bigley demanded. "Hell, we haven't even seen the Crandall woman, Charlie—"

"Excuse my contradiction," Chan interrupted, "but *you* have seen her—posing as her own sister. Look closely—ignore different hair and makeup of so-called Perkins, and you will see features of cleaning matron's fictional sister, Mrs. Baxter."

Mouth agape, the police detective stared at the woman. Recognition slowly dawned as Chan continued.

"Detective Bigley, you will recall visit to house of Baxter woman. If sisters were so close, so affectionate, one of them with children, why did Mrs. Baxter's sitting room have no family photographs—and no picture of two sisters together?

"Invention of a sister who frequently needed help provided convenient excuse for absences from hospital work," said Chan, returning his gaze to the silent Mrs. Perkins. "When you and husband realize that Notley must be silenced, you steal aboard *Monterey* to attempt murder there. But results uncertain—and faithless man may live to tell all. So you return unobserved to medical facility—cleaning staff knows best ways to arrive and depart from building in secret.

"You enter janitor's closet and remove sturdy strand from mop unused by lazy coworker Jenkins, strong enough to choke life from unconscious man in the room down the hall. But unfortunate janitor arrives unexpectedly, and you silence him with murder weapon already prepared for Notley.

"Wearing smock and cap of dead man you put idle mop to good use, cleaning your way toward Notley's room and entering unobserved to commit second murder. Laboratory confirmed my observation that dry mop strand found on closet floor was used to kill janitor—leaving no moisture on his neck—but after you used mop in hallway to approach Notley's room, similar strand was wet—and victim's neck showed traces of cleaning solution."

Chan paused, but no one spoke.

"You and deceased husband conspired for gain. Your hospital position provided information about women and their offspring, and when Notley posed threat you alone could gain access to closet containing murder weapon. You risked discovery, but you were confident—who looks closely at a cleaner mopping dirty floor?"

"But I saw Jenkins in the hall," protested Bigley. "You mean to tell me—"

"—that you saw *someone* wearing smock and hat, head down, applying wet mop vigorously to floor of hallway," Chan cut in. "You did not know janitor, but later we were told that he was on duty that day. Person you saw was this woman, who had already killed the unfortunate Jenkins with strand of mop—same mop from which she removed second strand to dispatch Notley."

"She sure looks like the Baxter woman, but how does that make her Marjorie Crandall as well?" Bigley said stubbornly. "I'm not tryin' to be disagreeable, Charlie, but Great Scott—"

"Skepticism is healthy quality for detective," Chan assured him. "So glad that Nurse Meadows is here to provide confirmation of this woman's identity."

The nurse had been staring at Mrs. Perkins for some little time as Charlie Chan spoke. Slowly, recognition turned to horror.

"How could you, Marj?" she cried. "What kind of monster are you?"

"Don't you fret none, dearie," mocked the voice of Marj Crandall from the lips of Mrs. Perkins. "No need to trouble yourself about me."

Abruptly the mask fell, and the woman abandoned all of her false personae.

"You silly fool," she snarled in something like her real voice. She turned toward Flannery, "If I'm under arrest, then I shouldn't have to sit here and listen to any more idiotic talk."

The deputy chief stood up abruptly.

"Oh, there's no 'if' about it, Mrs. Whoever-you-are," Flannery said firmly. "We're happy to oblige."

The deputy chief went to the door, opened it and nodded to a waiting duo of uniformed officers standing outside. Detective Bigley took the woman by the arm, none too gently, and turned her over to the waiting pair of patrolmen who escorted her from the room.

"I just can't believe it," Meadows whispered. "I thought I knew her—but she did those terrible things . . ." Her voice trailed off, and she covered her face in her hands.

Dr. Klindleman laid a gentle hand on the nurse's shoulder, murmured a few words of comfort, and turned toward Chan and the others.

"This has come as a terrible shock—to Nurse Meadows, naturally, but to me as well," he declared, looking pointedly at

Flannery. "I didn't know that—that—woman, whatever her name is, but assuming that she's guilty, then . . . what I'm trying to say is, you've arrested her, and I think Meadows and I . . . That is, if there's nothing more?"

The deputy chief sympathized. Dr. Klindleman was an eminent physician and a prominent community member.

"Charlie—Bigley?" Flannery got to his feet. "All right for these folks to go, since we're pretty much done here?"

Dr. K. and Nurse Meadows rose from the table, but Chan held up his hand.

"One moment, please. Overwhelmed with regret, I am forced to disagree with friend of many years." Chan's flowery words were uttered in a firm, no-nonsense tone. "Additional questions are necessary."

A mystified Flannery shrugged and sat down, and the two medical professionals resumed their seats.

"Nurse Meadows," the detective began, "you have many duties at hospital, caring for patients—preparing expectant mothers to welcome their offspring into the world."

"That's so, Mr. Chan," she agreed, smiling faintly. "It's a great deal of work, but the new moms and their little ones—that's what makes it all worthwhile."

Chan nodded.

"Valuable work—who could doubt it? Yet I believe sometimes you were asked to perform unusual tasks, maybe by superiors or others at hospital—perhaps small things, not normal hospital procedure."

It was a statement, not a question, but Chan paused and looked expectantly at the nurse. Meadows returned his gaze with a puzzled expression.

"I'm not sure I understand what you mean—I don't believe I was asked to do anything wrong," she said slowly. "I certainly wouldn't do anything that would jeopardize the health of my patients."

Chan bowed slightly in acknowledgement.

"I agree—your dedication is not in question," he replied. "Am referring to unusual method of record-keeping that involved small ink-mark on wrists of some mothers-to-be."

Nurse Meadows looked relieved.

"Oh, that! Yes, indeed, I was asked to make a little round mark—a kind of circle with two commas inside it, and two dots—on the wrists of some of the girls," she admitted. "And a similar mark on their chart, too." Her voice dropped. "It was quite sad, you see—these girls, some of them young women, were in a bad way, and their little ones would be candidates for an orphanage—for adoption, you understand."

Chan nodded.

"These patients—how did you know which should be marked so?"

"Every few days, a brief memo would indicate which newly admitted women fell into this—this category," the nurse explained. "When I began work at the hospital some years ago, it was explained to me that an informal method was used to avoid the complications of entering such unfortunate information into the official records. For the benefit of the girls—their situation wasn't always entirely their fault, you see—and the protection of the little ones."

"You believe this explanation of noble motives?" Chan asked blandly.

"At first, it did seem a bit unusual," the nurse admitted, "but we all know the stigma these women and their babies face, and the idea that one was doing something to help them—even this small thing—it made up for the one thing that—that troubled me."

Chan and the others at the table waited. Flannery was watching the proceedings closely. He knew of Charlie Chan's penchant for gradually revealing the solution to a complicated case and was certain that the detective from Hawaii was about to demonstrate it again. Bigley was trying to keep up, and Dr. Klindleman maintained his habitually benign expression.

Silence filled the room for a few seconds. The nurse sighed heavily but did not speak. Finally, the detective quietly prompted her to continue.

"This troublesome thing—maybe it was the fact that women who were 'unfortunate,' as you said, were also from particular part of the world?" Chan looked steadily at Meadows, who nodded sadly.

"The ones to be marked—they were supposed to have no husband or family, and they were to be from China or that part of the world," she said in a voice barely above a whisper. "It was the one aspect of the whole thing that I didn't understand, but a nurse's training—"

"The good nurse does as she is told," Chan put in. "Memos listing unfortunate women—who signed them?"

The nurse was nearly in tears now.

"They were just initialed," she said. "The whole thing had just become so routine, that I never gave it a second thought ." "But you and other nurses," Chan persisted, "you discussed patients—including these chosen patients. Others besides you knew?"

"A few of the girls, yes," Meadows admitted. "Especially after Mrs. Winterslip and the Jane Doe girl were both found to have family—that was very upsetting, but still—we all assumed that *he* knew better than we did, so we didn't question anything—"

"'He'?" Chan interjected.

The nurse looked at the eminent physician seated next to her.

"Why, Dr. Klindleman, of course."

Chapter Twenty-Five

"ONE HELL OF A NOISE"

C harlie Chan's face was impassive as he nodded and turned his attention toward the doctor. All eyes were on the eminent physician.

"You, Dr. Klindleman, enjoy a great reputation in San Francisco community for devotion to medical practice that serves mothers-to-be and the arrival of their offspring—even my own grandchild," the detective intoned. "Also, many praise your dedication to organizations that serve needy citizens, especially children without parents."

"That is so," the doctor acknowledged, "but it's my work—my research that's important, not I. Some in the community have been kind enough to take notice and have been supportive," he went on. "A number of them believe strongly in the work I hope to pursue in more depth."

"Through financial support?" Chan put in.

"Yes, although not enough to truly make a difference," Dr. Klindleman declared, warming to the subject. "Many, many people support my ideas, but the work requires much more financial support than has been forthcoming."

His face reddened slightly.

"If they would simply accept that we are on the verge of great changes, a whole new way of understanding mankind that will benefit those best suited to bring about a new age, a new era, then they would gladly provide the necessary dollars."

Chan's expression was unperturbed.

"You had urgent need to advance research far beyond unusual theories advanced by others—" Chan held up one of the texts he had borrowed "—and were willing to risk well-being of countless persons to gain large sums needed."

"I don't know what you're talking about," Dr. Klindleman retorted, his voice growing louder with each word. "I'm a man of science—"

"I think Miss Osogo can shed some light on this conversation," June Kirk interrupted. "As I mentioned, she has been working behind the scenes for some time."

"Thank you, Mrs. Kirk," Miss Osogo began, shifting her gaze from person to person as she addressed the gathering. "I will be brief, but please be assured that documentary evidence has been collected to support what I am telling you.

"Significant amounts of money have found their way into the finances of the Homeplace Orphanage—sums far in excess of the operational needs of the organization."

She paused for a moment.

"Dr. Klindleman serves on the Homeplace board of directors, and large transactions have been tracked—"

Dr. K. was not giving up without a fight.

"I've told you that attracting donations is necessary to advance the work, that is, the research, some of which involves the orphanage, and no doubt the financial activity you're describing represents some of that successful raising of funds," the doctor blustered.

Miss Osogo shook her head.

"No, Dr. Klindleman, my investigation shows and our office's analysis of your records will prove that you used Homeplace for your own purposes—including the illegal transfer of monies realized from the sale of dangerous contraband.

"In short, from the sale and distribution of certain illegal drugs. I would add," she continued over an attempted interruption from Dr. K., "that some of the currency that ended

up supporting your—er—research was easily tracked, because the larger denomination bills were marked.

"It's all here, in my report," she gestured toward a thick
bundle of documents, "but I think Inspector Chan has
something to add."

"Thank you, so much," Chan nodded. "Imperfect nun
makes excellent investigator.

"You were convinced of righteous cause," he began stern-
ly, turning his full attention toward the doctor. "Influenced
by misguided theories that would raise some above others,
you believed that criminal enterprise in support of noble
research was justified.

"Sometimes evil ideology wears mask of intellectual inquiry."

Dr. K.'s professional demeanor had faded, and his left eye
twitched. Bags and dark circles under both eyes spoke of
sleepless nights, and there was a slight but noticeable tremor
in the medical man's hands as he gestured emphatically.

"I tell you, no illegal activity happened that I was aware
of," he said deliberately. "Others may have acted improp-
erly, but I was not aware—"

Chan interrupted.

"On the contrary, police have confirmed that you were
fully aware that Mr. and Mrs. Huang received significant
sum to take charge of infant from orphanage intended for
evil fate, and were told to expect much larger sum after
returning to San Francisco with shipment of 'infant feeding
formula.'

"Interception of that shipment on Honolulu docks has
revealed that white powder masquerading as nutrition for
infants was dangerous drug to be distributed by organization you oversaw, to be sold by merchants of death,"
Chan asserted, "with large sums finding their way back to
you, through the orphanage—so that flawed research using
innocent persons could continue."

"You mischaracterize my research work and its intent," Dr. K. protested. "What do you—a mere policeman—know of such things? Why, some of the world's leading theorists in this field agree with me, and—and—governments as well?"Chan's eyes flashed.

"False science says millions of persons should be bred like cattle—some valued, others discarded," the detective's tone was merely terse, but his eyes narrowed in anger. "You instructed hospital staff to mark possible research subjects with ancient Chinese yin-yang symbol, and they did so without question because you were distinguished doctor. Some so-called experts write books about their theories, but you, Dr. Klindleman, experimented on mothers and their children.

"Fortunately, the woman recorded in hospital here as 'Jane Doe,' mother of infant in keeping of Mr. and Mrs. Huang, has been rescued from captivity in laboratory discovered by Honolulu police," Chan said, a recently received telegram in his grasp. "But others—how many others have you injured? How many of your experiments ended in death?

"Your crimes were evil beyond murder," Chan concluded. "You have much to answer for."

Dr. K.'s response was cut short by Deputy Chief Flannery, none too pleased at the doctor's characterization of a "mere policeman."

"I think we've heard enough. Detective Bigley, would you take Dr. Klindleman out of here?" Flannery's voice was tinged with disgust.

Bigley responded with alacrity, and the doctor found himself being propelled toward the door in an undignified manner.

"Am I under arrest?" Dr. K. shouted over his shoulder.

"Yes!" Flannery thundered. "And a long list of charges it will be, that's for sure."

A relative calm settled on the deputy chief's office, and the short-lived silence was broken by a teary Nurse Meadows.

"She was there—she heard me," she sobbed. She turned to Chan. "When your daughter was admitted, there was a mistake—it was thought that she was Rose Chan, a mother-to-be with no husband, no family. The doctor said we were not to mention it, that it might upset Mrs. Winterslip. And she, I mean, Marj Crandall, she heard me take the call and correct the record. She must've phoned the orphanage to tell them only one infant would be coming to them."

"Cleaning woman had access to telephone?" Chan said gently.

"She was always asking if she might use the phone at my station to check on her sister—so she said, anyway," Meadows wailed. "And there was a pay telephone near the end of the hall."

She turned her anguished face away, struggling to regain her composure.

"No doubt woman used phone to maintain communication with doctor and also orphanage," Chan said softly. "She must have called Virginia Lande, posing as nurse, to explain that only one infant was coming to Homeplace."

Bigley stirred; there was a lot for him to absorb.

"So this Lande—the orphanage director—?"

Chan shook his head.

"Operator of well-meaning institution trusted respectable doctor," he clarified. "Of Klindleman's dark motives for occasional housing and 'placement' of infants, she knew nothing."

Nurse Meadows stood up.

"If you have no questions for me—I'd like to leave now," she said in a choked voice. "This has been an awful shock, and I'd rather . . ."

As the woman's voice trailed off, a tear trickled down her cheek.

"Of course," June Kirk said sympathetically. "The police can reach you at the hospital if they need anything further—no objections, Tom? Charlie?"

Both men shook their heads and stood as Meadows exited the office, closing the door behind her.

Flannery exhaled noisily.

"Well, this is going to make one hell of a noise," he grumbled. "The sainted Dr. K.! From what you described, Charlie, San Francisco and Honolulu will have to figure out which gets to prosecute him first."

"I think our office can help with that, and I'm sure my boss will agree," Kirk offered. "Given the locations of the jurisdictions involved, it's clearly a federal case—but there will be plenty of legal work to go around, considering that the murders—"

"Yeah, those are strictly local," Flannery cut in. "Which reminds me, Charlie, what in blazes made you settle on this—this—whoever she is? And her choice of weapon?"

"For me it is difficult to separate murders, which came second, from contraband case, which came first—in the form of your request for consultation," Chan began his answer. "Deputy chief heard me compare one small clue to a grain of sand. Maybe meaningless when assembled with many other colored particles of sand to make complete picture, as ancient monks do in monasteries..

"As events grew in number, not just one small clue, but many small things began to appear, taking shape like grains of sand that begin to form finished image. While on board flying boat I encounter two nuns who eat meat on Friday. One who uses cosmetics—while the other seems to direct words toward me: 'place' and 'home.'

"Later," he nodded toward Flannery, "you delivered to me another grain of sand," he nodded toward Flannery, "dying informant's words. Significance was unknown to me then, but something clicked in aging detective's brain. And many more tiny particles were added to the growing picture as time went on."

Deputy Chief Flannery frowned.

"But why did this Perkins, or whatever his name was, risk approaching Henry—and you?" Flannery questioned. "First with Mrs. Perkins by his side he chats up Henry, then in his nun outfit he cozies up to you. Seems like he would've wanted to stay as far away as possible from the both of you."

"Two possibilities," Chan replied. "First, scheming Perkins may have sought to gather information and acquaint himself with detective to establish pretended innocence of his connections with orphanage and interest in its work. Second, actions of bold criminal suggest that he considered himself brilliant taker of risks—superior to dull-witted officials. Especially," he grinned, "aging Chinese detective.

"Ancient Greek philosopher had word for Mr. Perkins's behavior," said Chan. "*Hubris*."

The door opened, and Bigley rejoined the gathering.

"The good doctor is in a holding cell, and he'll be processed shortly," said the detective, dropping into a chair.

"Glad to hear it," Flannery said heartily. "Charlie was just filling us in on his thinking, so you're just in time to learn something from an old hand.

"Go ahead, Charlie," he urged. "The floor is still yours."

Chan delivered a nod that was almost a seated bow.

"I am humbled by the attention of all those who played important parts in bringing the guilty to justice," he said simply. "The honor is mine, and I thank you.

"Assembling clues," Chan reiterated for Bigley's benefit, "was like *mandala*—ancient practice of bringing together colored bits of sand to make picture. Each clue helps make complicated case simple, step by step," he continued, "so that at end we see the truth.

"Consider many more indications: Notley seeks conversation with son Henry, but fails to appear. Then, Notley's kit found with illegal drug present. Finally, Notley survives attack on board ship only to die at hands of mysterious hospital killer who has already silenced co-worker not far away.

"Buying and selling and smuggling of dangerous drugs, two deaths in same hospital so near to one another. Woman in maternity wing who disappears after encounter with my daughter—both marked on wrist for some purpose. Cleaning matron who cannot be found, sister who lives in isolation—and orphanage where preparations are made for two, then one infant—all these told small parts of story.

"All these clues, like grains of sand forming big picture," Chan said grimly, "came together to reveal brilliant, proud medical man who ruined lives to finance sinister research."

"I'll remind you that we poor policemen," Flannery began, with a wave of his hand that included Bigley as well as himself, "cops that pounded a beat to start out, we didn't have a lot of time to keep up with modern science."

June Kirk suppressed a smile. She knew that Flannery possessed a keen intellect—even though he lacked the academic credentials to prove it.

The deputy chief wiped his forehead with a handkerchief drawn from a uniform pocket.

"All this by way of saying, Charlie, just what the hell was Dr. K. researching? Why did he need these women and their babies?"

Chan's eyes narrowed.

"Examination of books from doctor's office pointed to branch of so-called science named 'eugenics' by those who believe in it. This Klindleman's explorations began with study of research on plants—"

"The little book you were readin'!" Bigley broke in. "Something about onions—"

Chan nodded.

"That author's early research interest in dividing of onion root cells was legitimate," the detective went on, "but he and others whose works occupied Dr. K.'s shelves followed dark path, promoting eugenics as way of proving human qualities superior in one race above all others."

Flannery opened his mouth to speak, but Chan continued hurriedly.

"Astute colleague asks pointed question: Why these women, some expecting arrival of offspring and others having recently delivered same? No doubt this Dr. Klindleman will explain in courtroom his distorted reasoning for comparisons of women and newborns of Asian blood with other subjects—maybe unlucky victims from many parts of world. Honolulu police even now have started to explore sinister laboratory for evidence.

"Unfortunately," Chan concluded, "this doctor's views are shared by like-minded scientists and even some governments—especially those that seek to eliminate so-called inferior persons to achieve warped vision."

No one spoke for several seconds. Recent events abroad came to mind for those around the table. The newspapers of late made for difficult reading.

"*Kē zhèng měng yú hǔ*," Chan said under his breath. "Cruel governments are more dangerous than fierce tigers."

Chapter Twenty-Six

PASSAGE FOR TWO

Flannery cleared his throat. Over the years, he had developed great respect for Charlie Chan, but the deputy chief considered himself a simple and straightforward cop.

"I've learned to trust you, Charlie," he said, "because you always come through in the end. Whatever else he was up to, I leave that to your department and June's boss. But Klindleman—the 'great Dr. K.'—involved in the drug trade? That's going to be a lot for some people to swallow, including members of a jury."

Chan smiled broadly.

"This consultant is pleased to submit theory of case to proper authorities," he said happily. "I am confident that skilled interrogators of suspected persons will arrive at credible testimonies for prosecution of guilty persons.

"Great doctor will blame underlings for murders and other criminal actions, and he will cling to his discredited science as a defense, but evidence will show his so-called research depended on kidnapping unwilling persons and disposing of them after their use to him was ended. All made possible by sums of money from sale of illicit substances, proceeds of which enriched criminal enterprise maintained by the Perkins couple."

"That part of the picture seems clear to me," Flannery agreed. "But how many other people were involved—hospital staff, for example?"

"Some may have been willing participants," replied Chan, "but others could have performed tasks without knowing whole picture. For example, they transported expectant women from place to place and kept informal records. Respect for doctor's reputation no doubt convinced many that he could do no wrong.

"In assisting capable San Francisco colleagues," Chan finished with a grin, "I wanted to leave some work undone—for young Bigley and others eager to build their careers. They will find many who are willing to talk, and in my experience threat of cage makes birds sing willingly—even at the expense of head bird."

Laughter adjourned the meeting, but Charlie Chan observed a quiet exchange of words between his son and June Kirk as the others made their way out of the room. The detective smiled. He was not surprised.

After hospital protocols pertaining to recovery from childbearing had been satisfied, Rose Winterslip and daughter were discharged and happily transported by John Quincy to the Winterslip home. Despite the joyous occasion the new father had old business on his mind.

"Charlie—esteemed father-in-law, I mean," John Quincy began. "Say, neither of those forms of address seems appropriate, do they? Anyway, Rose may have forgotten this, but I've been wanting to ask you about the markings on her wrist and the other woman's. What was the point of that, when the unfortunate women they targeted could be easily recognized?"

"Your keen mind probes deeper even than Deputy Chief Flannery's," Chan grinned. "Earlier I explained that markings were crude versions of ancient Chinese concept—same symbol Detective Bigley and I saw in Dr. Klindleman's office. Philosophers count several meanings of two shapes that oppose each other but also complete each other. Like darkness and light, one cannot exist without the other.

"Only infamous doctor could explain his reason for use of yin-yang," the detective concluded.

"Come on, Charlie—you must have a theory!" Winterslip smiled. "What's your best guess?"

"Not a guess, but I can offer possibilities," Chan returned. "Likely but not certain that Dr. Klindleman chose to mark women with symbol that he displayed in his office. Maybe he thought philosophy of long ago justified his misguided efforts. Many have sought to balance humanity in some way, in peace and war. Doctor thought his misguided research could do so, and he saw discarding humans in research as a necessary evil—one that would lead to greater good.

"But marking patients could have been done by some other person involved in this conspiracy, one unaware of yin-yang's complex meanings.

"Whoever was responsible party wanted to indicate that chosen ones were to be part of so-called research without putting criminal action into writing," he continued. "Appearance of women was not enough to ensure that correct subjects were taken from hospital.

"In fact," Chan said solemnly, "both Rose and Jane Doe were fortunate to have escaped cruel fate that claimed other women chosen in doctor's scheme."

"I'll say!" John Quincy replied fervently. "I don't want to dwell on the whole thing, but I guess it all made sense—to a crook, maybe," he mused. "But even their unwritten method failed in two cases that we know of—"

"Method designed by man destined to fail," his father-in-law pointed out. "One or more persons involved in chain of selection thought both Rose and Jane Doe had no friends, no families," Chan said. "Fortunate that Rose woke up speaking English. Not so for Jane Doe, who relied mostly on native tongue. Still, she could read enough English to understand chart—pointing out Chan name to Rose.

"Then angry mother of Jane Doe confronts doctor in hallway, and he tells panicked lies to conceal second failure of scheme. Thanks to Henry reporting conversation he overheard, Jane Doe—real name, Liao Tsuifeng—and baby daughter now restored to new grandmother and other family members.

"Actions of brave women helped bring down criminal enterprise like lighting lamp chases away darkness."

With Henry and his parents in temporary residence, Chans outnumbered Winterslips in the happy household, but John Quincy's storied family was not forgotten. His mother's latest telegram had arrived minutes after the newly enlarged family crossed the threshold:

JOY AT ARRIVAL OF GRANDCHILD TOO GREAT FOR MERE TELEGRAM STOP PLEASE ADVISE WHETHER YOU PREFER TWO HOUSE GUESTS OR FAMILY TRIP TO BOSTON STOP AUNT MINERVA AND I ALREADY PACKED STOP SHE JOINS ME IN SENDING UNLIMITED

LOVE
MOTHER

"Well!" John Quincy exclaimed. "Mother doesn't let the grass grow or moss form or whatever metaphor you prefer. What say you to this Hobson's choice, my dear?"

Rose sighed contentedly. Babe in arms, the new mother sat in the first domestic chair she had occupied in several days. She was looking forward to resuming a diet of "real" food.

"I'm so happy to be home," she murmured. "The thought of a long trip right now . . . on the other hand we already have house guests, and—"

"Two of whom will soon beg leave to depart," her father reminded her. "Circumstances that permitted lengthy absence from official police duties now resolved, and Chief will expect my return to same.

"Perhaps Henry will accompany aged parent on voyage while new grandmother awaits arrival of Boston counterpart," Chan suggested. Secretly, he was much amused at the prospect of the impending matriarchal "East Meets West" in a domestic setting—one in which neither grandmother would be in charge.

"But you'll be back soon, won't you Dad?" Rose Winterslip said wistfully. "You'll want to see your little granddaughter often, won't you?"

"Does a wise man argue with a woman?" Chan grinned. "Grandparents will visit soon and often so they can observe little one called—"

"I thought you'd never ask!" John Quincy interrupted gleefully. "We wanted to wait till we were home before announcing your granddaughter's name." Rose nodded, jogging the baby gently back and forth.

"Her name is June Grace Chan Winterslip, officially," the new mother said proudly, "but I think we'll call her Gracie."

The next few days flew by as parents, grandparents, uncle and family friends doted on Gracie.

Among the congratulatory cards that arrived in the mail was a gracious note from the family of Chan Kee Lim, Charlie Chan's San Francisco cousin, whom the detective had called on during past visits to the city. *No time to visit ancient cousin this time*, he reflected. *Maybe next trip to mainland.* Eager to return to work Chan had already booked passage for two on the *Lurline*, the first available liner sailing for Honolulu.

After a farewell family luncheon, Henry helped load the detective's luggage into a waiting taxi for the drive to the pier as the rest of the family exchanged embraces and cries of "Aloha" with father and son.

Sensing an uneasiness in his oldest son Charlie Chan sought to pour oil on troubled waters.

"In haste of discussing conclusion of case with authorities I neglected to point out your part in investigation," he began. "Talent and ability did not go unnoticed by me—you rose to each challenge and overcame it."

"Thanks, Dad," Henry said gratefully. "I was glad to do my part. I think I appreciate more than ever just how hard your job is . . . especially all the times I thought I was onto something—"

"—only to experience sudden course correction," his father finished. "Best indication of budding skills was your ability to adjust to circumstances, such as crewman Notley's frantic attempts to betray criminal enterprise."

"That reminds me," Henry replied. "Why couldn't he just come across with the information instead of trying to arrange a meeting?"

Chan sighed.

"Here you encountered any detective's greatest challenge—unpredictability of human heart. This Notley, he knew right from wrong but feared retribution. Rightly so, as he discovered too late. Yet real or imagined threats stilled his tongue: first on ship, then at dark meeting where he could have spoken truth. There, he senses he is watched and delays talk till later meeting that never happens.

"Even in hospital he made one last attempt to leave clue of evil activity that most troubled him—gripping nurse by the arm to impress the word 'baby' on her ears."

"I didn't know he had done that," Henry admitted. "But why did he take such a risk by trying to meet me at Calico Jim's? And why didn't he show?"

"Nervous Notley's motives known only to him," Chan pointed out, "but likely causes of behavior are several. Anxious to find a way out of criminal gang, he planned to meet you outside of tavern to show you vital parts of whole enterprise."

"Calico Jim's and the warehouse behind it," Henry put it. "And Moran didn't want me leaving by the back door because—"

"Warehouse served as way station for drugs," Chan continued, "and sometimes unfortunate women and infants.

"Notley's failure to keep rendezvous caused by several influences," the detective went on. "Discovery of drugs in his kit on Monterey suggests that he had given in to temptation and was slave to evil habit—nervous behavior suggests same—and effects of drug use were compounded by threats and, finally, fatal lack of courage.

"As in, 'He who hesitates is lost,'" quoted Henry. "I guess that old saying really sums up poor Notley."

"Chinese put it more eloquently," Chan countered, "The venerable Lieu-Tzu, for example—"

"Where is your suitcase, Henry?" his mother demanded. "Quick, get bag from house or you will miss taxi and boat and—"

Henry took a deep breath before replying.

"Mama, Dad, I'm—I'm not sailing today."

Mama Chan was stunned and silent, but only for a moment. She launched into a torrent of Cantonese but was soon interrupted by Charlie Chan's soothing words.

"Please, Mama, allow Henry to explain the offer of employment that awaits him here," the detective said blandly.

Henry stared at his father, but he wasn't surprised.

"No use trying to spring something on you, is there, Dad?" Henry grinned in defeat. "I'll bet you know all about it."

"Only know from observation of your quiet conversation with June Kirk after recent meeting that something was 'in the works,' as you would say," his father countered. "Hunch tells me that your interest in detection and chance to demonstrate mature action in face of danger make you ideal candidate for investigative position with her office, yes?"

"A junior investigator position with her office, yes," the younger Chan admitted. "She said from what she's seen, combined with whatever ability I may have inherited, that I am more than qualified. Also—"

"Also maybe you welcome the opportunity to work in same office with former 'wife' Lily?" Charlie Chan said mischievously. "All work and no play—"

"Let's not get ahead of ourselves, Dad," Henry objected feebly, his face reddening despite his best efforts. "It's true that Lily and I hit it off, but—"

Fortunately for Henry, other family members interrupted the father-son sparring to offer their congratulations. Chan embraced his wife and daughter, tweaked the chin of his granddaughter and entered the taxi whose driver waited impassively.

"Aloha, beloved family," Charlie Chan called out as he waved through the open window. "Until we meet again, aloha."

THE END

ACKNOWLEDGEMENTS

My thanks to all those who have embraced the *Charlie Chan Returns* series: readers, reviewers, old friends and new. As always, the encouragement of my academic author-spouse Patricia Swann sustains my efforts; and the unique cover art is the work of my talented daughter Sarah K. Swann. Nick Burns continues to bring to bear his years of publishing and marketing expertise, and NKB Publishing's role in the revival of a beloved fictional character cannot be overstated.

None of this would be possible, of course, without the author Earl Derr Biggers and Chinese-Hawaiian detective Chang Apana, whose remarkable career provided the inspiration for the creation of Charlie Chan.

ABOUT THE AUTHOR

Former broadcast journalist John L. Swann lives in an old house on a hill in Upstate New York with his wife, Patricia, whose years of gentle prodding resulted in his writing new Charlie Chan mysteries. When not plotting the next book in the series, he enjoys playing a rickety upright piano that's older than Chan and noodling on a ukulele.

Read the first two mysteries in our series
Charlie Chan Returns

Death, I Said
Violence and death upend a
quiet university campus in
1930s San Francisco.

The Tangled String
Thievery, death, and
blue-blooded family
skeletons at a Boston hotel.

With wit, wisdom, and intuitive intellect, Charlie Chan will
crack the case and unmask the guilty. Available at
Amazon.com, BarnesAndNoble.com, and booksellers
everywhere.